From murderers to missing babies to a shaggy dog with an unusual appetite, openly gay Honolulu homicide detective Kimo Kanapa'aka has his hands full in this selection of ten short investigations in the Aloha State. Sun-drenched streets hide bodies in their shadows and clues lurk in the most unusual places, from a hearse to a flowering hedge to a psychic who provides Kimo with an unexpected revelation. These sexy, smart and satisfying stories will please new readers and fans of the Mahu series as well.

D1594630

# MLR PRESS AUTHORS

Featuring a roll call of some of the best writers of gay erotica and mysteries today!

| | | |
|---|---|---|
| Derek Adams | Kyle Adams | Vicktor Alexander |
| Z. Allora | Simone Anderson | Victor J. Banis |
| Laura Baumbach | Ally Blue | J.P. Bowie |
| Barry Brennessel | Jade Buchanan | James Buchanan |
| TA Chase | Charlie Cochrane | Karenna Colcroft |
| Jamie Craig | Ethan Day | Diana DeRicci |
| Vivien Dean | Taylor V. Donovan | S.J. Frost |
| Kimberly Gardner | Kaje Harper | Stephani Hecht |
| Alex Ironrod | Jambrea Jo Jones | DC Juris |
| AC Katt | Thomas Kearnes | Kiernan Kelly |
| K-lee Klein | Geoffrey Knight | Christopher Koehler |
| Matthew Lang | J.L. Langley | Vincent Lardo |
| Cameron Lawton | Anna Lee | Elizabeth Lister |
| William Maltese | Z.A. Maxfield | Timothy McGivney |
| Kendall McKenna | AKM Miles | Robert Moore |
| Reiko Morgan | Jet Mykles | Jackie Nacht |
| N.J. Nielsen | Cherie Noel | Gregory L. Norris |
| Willa Okati | Erica Pike | Neil S. Plakcy |
| Rick R. Reed | A.M. Riley | AJ Rose |
| Rob Rosen | George Seaton | Riley Shane |
| Jardonn Smith | DH Starr | Richard Stevenson |
| Christopher Stone | Liz Strange | Marshall Thornton |
| Lex Valentine | Haley Walsh | Mia Watts |
| Lynley Wayne | Missy Welsh | Ryal Woods |
| Stevie Woods | Sara York | Lance Zarimba |
| Mark Zubro | | |

*Check out titles, both available and forthcoming, at*
*www.mlrpress.com*

# ACCIDENTAL CONTACT AND OTHER MAHU INVESTIGATIONS

NEIL S. PLAKCY

**mlr**press

*www.mlrpress.com*

Copyright 2014 by Neil Plakcy

Published by
MLR Press, LLC
3052 Gaines Waterport Rd.
Albion, NY 14411

Visit ManLoveRomance Press, LLC on the Internet:
www.mlrpress.com

Cover Art by Kris Jacen
Editing by Kris Jacen

Print format: ISBN# 978-1-60820-951-4
ebook format also available

Issued 2014

Introduction ...................................................................... 1

Accidental Contact ............................................................ 5

Kelly Green ...................................................................... 21

Refuge .............................................................................. 39

A Shaggy Dog Story ......................................................... 49

Macadamia Nuts to You .................................................. 63

Body Removal ................................................................... 79

The Burning Woman ....................................................... 101

Other People's Children .................................................. 113

Alpha and Omega ........................................................... 133

Transmission .................................................................... 157

Acknowledgements .......................................................... 189

# Introduction

I wrote my first short story about Kimo Kanapa'aka a few months after I had completed the fourth—or maybe the fifth—draft of *Mahu*, the first novel in what has turned out to be a long series. Kimo wouldn't let go of my imagination, but I was determined not to spend another year writing a second novel about him without knowing if the first would ever be published.

So I began a short story instead. I had begun to consider that *Mahu* was the first step in his coming-out process, and I was interested in exploring what would happen next for him. Once he'd come out to his family, and on the job, how would his life change? And how would that affect the cases that he investigated?

While I waited to see if *Mahu* would sell to a publisher (this was back in the early 2000s, before the advent of ebooks and self-publishing) I started to write stories that focused on what I called "the danger of the closet." Men who were forced into difficult or dangerous situations because they couldn't, or wouldn't, admit to their true sexual desires. I also played around with the idea that after his very public coming-out story, lots of gay men in Hawai'i would know who he was.

Eventually, *Mahu* did sell, to Haworth Press, and I plunged into writing a second book in the series. But ideas kept coming to me. Some of them weren't big enough to merit a whole book, so I continued to write stories.

I keep pretty close track of when the stories and books happen in Kimo's timeline, and I've included a complete timeline for the stories and books so far at the end of this collection. The first two stories here, "Accidental Contact" and "Refuge," happen between *Mahu Fire* and *Mahu Vice*, during a time when Kimo and his eventual partner, fire investigator Mike Riccardi, are not seeing each other.

SPOILER ALERT!

It's important (to me, at least) to point out here that soon after *Mahu Fire*, when Kimo and Mike meet and fall in love, Mike lies to Kimo about something he's done, and they break up. At the time, I couldn't see how these two guys could stay together, because it was the first serious relationship for each of them. I even had a new boyfriend in mind for Kimo, a slightly older architect whom Kimo would meet in an investigation of the death of the architect's lover.

That story never got written, though, because Kimo was still in love with Mike, and he let me know that he wanted a chance to try again. I thought that the break would be a good chance for them both to fool around, see what dating was like, and recognize how much they meant to each other.

END SPOILER

I'm a magpie when it comes to character details and story ideas. A news item, a bumper sticker on a passing car, or a casual comment from a friend can all spark my imagination. The first story in this collection, "Accidental Contact," arose from an online report of a similar incident at a hospital somewhere. I had the same reaction to the story that Kimo has—that my penis had never "accidentally" come in contact with someone else's mouth, or vice versa.

Though there's no such place as the QuickStop in Kahala, there's a 7-Eleven in my hometown in Pennsylvania, and at least twice I've run into men in kelly green pants there, buying ice. I went through my own period of kelly green pants and pink polo shirts with popped collars, so I knew that world and was interested to expose Kimo to it.

"Refuge" was inspired by my own trip to the Pu`uhonua O Hōnaunau National Historical Park on the Big Island. Because of how long it took to actually get *Mahu* published, this story was Kimo's first exposure to the real world. I read an excerpt from it at an open reading at the Behind Our Masks gay lit convention in Washington DC in 1998. A friend I made there later was a guest editor for the online magazine *Blithe House Quarterly*, and he accepted the story for publication there in the Spring 2000 edition.

For twelve years, I was privileged to share my life with a seventy-plus pound shaggy dog, a golden retriever named Samwise who loved to jump up and hug me around the waist with his big paws. Of course, that put his nose level with my crotch and he did what dogs do; he sniffed. But what if a dog did more than that?

According to the TV Tropes website, a "Shaggy Dog Story is a plot with a high level of build-up and complicating action, only to be resolved with an anti-climax or ironic reversal, usually one that makes the entire story meaningless." Using that idea as my inspiration, I came up with "A Shaggy Dog Story," which also offers a bit of homage to the sexy noir novels written by my good friend Vicki Hendricks.

One of my favorite stories to write was "Macadamia Nuts to You." My good friend Anthony Bidulka was kind enough to give Kimo a cameo appearance in his novel *Aloha Candy Hearts*. To return the favor, I wrote this story, with Tony's input. Both sides of the process were fascinating—to see Kimo through another author's eyes, and also to take Russell Quant and portray him in a way that would be consistent with Tony's work. Even the title is a reference to Tony's practice of including food items in his book titles.

Special thanks goes to Cindy Chow, librarian and book reviewer extraordinaire, who took me to Kailua and showed me the farmer's market there.

One of the great benefits of belonging to the Florida chapter of Mystery Writers of America is the opportunity to attend monthly luncheons. A couple of years ago, my friend Miriam Auerbach invited her brother-in-law, a funeral director, to tell us some behind-the-scenes stories, and when I learned about the places you could hide something in a hearse, I was inspired to write "Body Removal."

Living in Florida, I often see people sprawled out on beach chairs sleeping in the sun. But what if one of those people wasn't sleeping—but was dead? "The Burning Woman" came out of that "what if."

With "Other People's Children" and "Alpha and Omega" I was inspired by Kimo and Mike's journey toward fatherhood. I resisted this impulse of theirs for as long as I could—I don't have kids myself, and didn't want to get sucked into writing something I knew nothing about. But becoming dads seemed clearly to be the next step for them, so I gave in. Another news article—this one about a young woman who no one knew was pregnant until she gave birth—spurred me to consider how someone could steal that baby. I'd also long had an interest in the Hawaiian tradition of the "'amakua," or spirit animal, and had been waiting for a way to bring Kimo's 'amakua into a story.

The timing didn't work out for Kimo and Mike's twins, Addie and Owen, to be born during a novel. I've tried to keep those books happening in close to real time, about a year apart. But I knew that fans would want to see the birth. I cast around for a way to tell that story but wrap a mystery around it. That's when I realized that though I mentioned Kimo's white grandmother, who had come to the islands as a missionary, I'd never explored her story. It was fascinating to put myself back in time and consider what had driven her to the islands, and how she had come to marry Kimo's grandfather.

The final story in the collection reflects my interest in Kimo's family and in what happens to them between the major cases. When I first began writing about Kimo, I made the mistake (hah!) of giving him a large family, including many nieces and nephews. As the series has progressed, and Kimo has aged, so have all those kids. And now that they are old enough to get into real trouble, I've grown more and more interested in them.

"Transmission" mixes the death of a teenager with the more standard troubles that Kimo's nieces and nephews are getting into—issues of sex, relationships, education and independence—and I hope show that by being an uncle he is growing into being a dad as well.

The words to the Joni Mitchell song about paradise being paved were running through my mind as I drove my truck from Waikiki into downtown Honolulu on a crisp winter Tuesday morning. The sun shone brightly over the green mass of the Ko'olau mountains and palm trees swayed in a gentle breeze. But everywhere I looked, construction cranes had sprung up, like giant monsters devouring the landscape.

My radio crackled to life when I was still a few blocks away from my office at the Honolulu Police Department, where I was the only openly gay homicide detective. It wasn't a distinction I aimed for, but rather one that was thrust upon me, one I tried to honor as much as I could.

Dispatch directed me to an alley off Lauhala Street, in the shadow of the H1 highway, where the body of an unidentified male had been found in a construction dumpster. It was a few blocks past police headquarters down South Beretania Street, and as I passed the four-story building, I thought ruefully of all the paperwork on my desk that I still wasn't going to get finished.

I pulled up behind a patrol car on Lauhala, next to a medical office building under construction by The Queen's Medical Center. The sun was rising over Mount Tantalus and the central business district was beginning its day. The weatherman had promised us rain later in the day, but the trade winds were blowing off the ocean and there wasn't a cloud in the sky.

The responding officer was Lidia Portuondo, a no-nonsense patrol officer I had known for years. Her dark hair was coiled in a bun, her uniform neat and crisp. "What have we got?" I asked, as I walked to where she stood talking to a scruffy-looking guy who I guessed was Samoan, about six-four and close to 350 pounds.

To the Samoan man, she said, "This is Detective Kanapa'aka, from homicide." Then she turned to me. "Morning, Kimo. Mr.

Momoa here is a laborer on the site over there." She motioned toward the half-built building. A four-story steel skeleton had been clad in concrete block, and a flat corrugated steel roof was in place. I could see that they had already begun framing out the office space on the first floor with metal studs and drywall.

"I clean up before the guys get started," Momoa said. "At night, stuff blows around in the wind, and sometimes kids or bums get in. I took a load of stuff out to the dumpster. I get the lid up, and I'm about to pour the crap in when I see the guy there."

"A Filipino male, approximately forty years of age, resting on his side," Lidia said. "Big stab wound to the back. Noted this thing, might be the weapon, next to the body."

"What do you mean, thing?"

She shrugged. "I don't know what to call it."

"Show me."

She and Momoa walked me over to the dumpster, which had been propped open. The crime scene team arrived, so she went to brief them, and I stepped up to the dumpster and looked inside. The body lay on a bed of drywall debris, the legs curled in a partial fetal position. Next to it was the bloody weapon Lidia had mentioned.

I recognized it immediately. When I was a teenager I spent my summers working for my father, a general contractor. I did everything from cleaning up, like Momoa, to hanging drywall, and I could still recognize the sharp-pointed rigid blade of a wallboard saw. It was used for things like cutting out a hole in drywall for an electrical outlet or phone jack.

I stepped back from the dumpster and let the crime scene techs do their work. I called the ME's office and asked them to send out a wagon, then took a detailed statement from Momoa, finding out he had left the site the day before at three-thirty. A number of carpenters had still been working when he left.

Then I joined Lidia in taking statements from each of the other workers—what time they had left the day before, had they seen anyone around the site, and so on. It was tedious work, and the cool morning air burned off quickly. Even in a blue-and-white aloha shirt, khakis, and deck shoes without socks, I was roasting. I moved the interviews to the shade of a big kukui tree, but that didn't help much.

When the ME's van arrived, Doc Takayama was with them. "Slow day today?" I asked. It was rare that our ME came out for anything less than a high-profile homicide. Then I saw the way he was looking at Lidia and it clicked. I'd had a feeling the two had a relationship that was more than professional.

"Just wanted to get out in the sunshine for a few minutes," Doc said. He was carrying a short yellow plastic stool that I wondered about. Was it part of some new forensic technique?

I watched as he walked over to the dumpster, where he met and talked to Lidia. Then she gave him a leg up and he climbed into the dumpster with his plastic stool. I stood in the shade of the kukui and waited until his head popped up again. I realized he'd carried the stool into the dumpster with him so he'd have a way to get out. The things you learn working with a pathologist.

I walked over to him as he was peeling off his blue rubber gloves. "You have anything for me yet?"

"From the angle of entry, the victim was most likely kneeling on the floor, the knife thrust into his back from above," he said. He still looked incongruously young to me, though at thirty-two we were the same age. Doc, however, had already gone through medical school, a residency, and internship, as well as a fellowship in pathology at Claremont. He joked that he had chosen to be an ME because his patients couldn't complain about how young he looked.

"Consistent with someone begging for his life?" I asked.

"That would be a reasonable interpretation," Doc said.

"And any idea about time of death?"

"Without opening him up, I can only say sometime in the last twelve to eighteen hours. I'll try and narrow that gap once I see what's what."

His techs lifted the body out of the dumpster and waited while I took a bunch of digital photos of the victim's face. He was neatly dressed, in lightweight scrubs and an orange t-shirt that read "Hug a Pineapple." No wallet or other identification. His shoes were interesting; white, rubber-soled clogs, which made me think he was a nurse at Queen's, that perhaps he'd been mugged leaving work the night before.

Once the techs were gone and the carpenters had all gone back to work, I headed for the cool, air-conditioned interior of the medical center. I started at the security office, but no on one duty recognized the victim's photo. After trying a couple of floors, I found a haole, or white, woman in the medical-surgical unit who said, "Oh, my God, that's Miguel," covering her mouth with her hand.

"I'm sorry," I said. "Do you know Miguel's last name?"

"Bohulano. Oh my God, he's dead, isn't he?"

I asked her to spell the name. "We worked together sometimes, but not recently," she said. "Let me check the computer." She leaned toward the monitor and hit a couple of keys. "He was on yesterday from seven a.m. to three-thirty p.m. Marta was here, too."

She introduced me to Marta, a young Filipina nurse. "He say anything about where he was going after work?" I asked.

She shook her head. Miguel was a sweet guy, she said, always cracking jokes and singing funny songs in Tagalog. Patients liked him. He was neat and his case notes were clear. No one else I spoke to on the floor had much else to contribute.

I went to the personnel office and spoke with a middle-aged Chinese woman named Helen Lau. She looked up his records on her computer. "He's originally from the Philippines," she said. "He went to nursing school there, and he had a current nursing license."

"Next of kin?"

She gave me an address for his mother in Quezon City.

"How long had he worked here?"

"According to this, just under a year," she said.

I asked what kind of employee he had been. She was apologetic; it was hospital policy not to divulge anything from an employee's personnel file without a court order, even in a case like this, where the records might help lead to his murderer.

"There is one thing I can tell you," she said. "Good nurses are hard to find, and hospitals work hard to hold on to them. Mr. Bohulano's record indicates he moved around a lot more frequently than a good nurse would. When you get the subpoena for our records, get one for each of the places he worked before, too."

I wrote down the information I needed, thanked her, and said I'd be back when I had the paperwork. By the time I got downstairs, the rain the weatherman had predicted had arrived, a heavy shower that lasted only long enough to drench me as I ran to my truck.

It was already past lunchtime, so I grabbed some takeout to eat at my desk while I put together the information the DA's office would need for the subpoenas. While I waited for them, I finished the paperwork on a couple of outstanding cases—a college girl shot by a jealous boyfriend as she came out of the downtown office building where she had a part-time job, and a tourist knifed in a late-night mugging a few blocks from the Aloha Tower.

By the end of my shift I didn't have anything new—the ME's report wouldn't come through 'til the next day, and the DA's office was still processing all those subpoenas. The weather had cleared up, so after I drove back to my apartment in Waikiki, I pulled out my surfboard and walked down to Kuhio Beach Park.

The longer I remained a homicide detective, the harder it got to contemplate the parade of victims, and surfing was the only way I could stay sane. Outside the breakers, I focused on watching the waves, choosing the one that would carry me to shore. I could forget the senseless deaths, the innocent and guilty victims, the pain of those left behind.

The beach was crowded and it was hard to catch a good wave, and as the sunset cruises began to leave with their colorful sails unfurled, I rode one last wave to the shore. I walked up the sand toward home, but like a homing beacon, I felt the Rod and Reel Club signaling to me.

You'd think I would stay away from the place, after the trouble I had run into there in the past, but it was the closest gay bar to my apartment, and the bartender let me run a tab. It was a friendly place, and the mix of gay and straight patrons made it easier for me as I took my first steps out of the closet. I'd met other guys there who felt the same way.

Still damp, I pulled up a stool at the bar and ordered a Longboard Lager. It was the tail end of happy hour, and the patio wasn't too crowded. A couple of tourist clusters filled the round tables, and a smattering of gay men sat at the bar or lounged in small groups under the big kukui tree. I didn't see anyone I knew, or anyone I wanted to know, so I finished my beer and went home.

Wednesday morning I was at my desk at seven. The DA's office had prepared the subpoenas and gotten them signed late the day before, and then faxed them to the appropriate hospitals. Our department fax started ringing with their responses, and I spent most of the morning looking at Miguel Bohulano's personnel records.

At each hospital, male patients had complained of inappropriate touching, often when they were partially sedated. And in each case, Bohulano had first been disciplined, then warned, then finally fired. But because of the confidentiality of personnel records, the next hospital down the chain knew nothing of his previous problems. At Queen's, he was already on probation for two offenses. In one case, his statement read that his mouth had "accidentally" come in contact with the patient's penis while Bohulano was changing a dressing on the man's leg.

Thinking back on all my sexual experiences, I knew my mouth had never "accidentally" come in contact with another man's penis, nor vice versa. I looked at the employee photos that had been faxed over as part of Bohulano's records; he wasn't a bad-looking guy. A bit skinny and ten years too old for my taste, but there were certainly enough rice queens—non-Asian men who preferred Asian male lovers—in Honolulu to keep him busy on a Saturday night. Or sticky guys—Asian men who liked Asians.

I sat back in my chair to contemplate Miguel Bohulano's life. He grew up in Quezon City and went to nursing school in Manila. Had he been abused as a boy? How had he come to associate power with sex? Surely in jerking off male patients under their flimsy gowns, he was asserting his power over them. A clear abuse of his ethics as a nurse—as well as behavior that was unlikely to result in the patient asking him out on a date.

There was no way to find out what had happened in his childhood; the only person who might have a clue was his mother, and he probably never told her anything about it. He had left the Philippines ten years before, and I had no doubt that patient abuse had caused his departure. I didn't know what privacy laws were like in the Philippines, but it was possible he'd been blacklisted for an incident, or else had simply seen the handwriting on the wall and left for Hawai'i.

In the last ten years he had worked for five different hospitals, each one passing him on to the next employer without a negative word. Indeed, the folders were filled with praise—he was skilled, caring, a patient favorite—except for those complaints.

Because I'm a cop, and I look for patterns, I went back over the incident reports. Had Miguel Bohulano picked a particular type of guy—by age, ethnicity, ailment? I couldn't find one. A couple of the victims self-identified in their complaint as gay, while several others made a point of asserting their heterosexuality. Another group made no mention.

Shortly after noon, the ME's report came in. It confirmed everything Doc had told me the morning before—Bohulano had been on his knees, and the knife blow to his back had come from above. The wallboard saw was the weapon, but the killer must have used work gloves, because there were no prints on it.

One fact stood out. Traces of dried semen had been found around Bohulano's mouth. I picked up the phone and dialed the morgue. After I bantered for a few minutes with his merry receptionist, Doc came on the line. "The position of the victim and the murderer," I said. "Is that also consistent with the possibility that Bohulano had just given a blow job?"

"I thought you'd come to that conclusion, detective," he said. "That hypothesis is supported by the presence of dried semen at the edge of the victim's lip. I put the DNA sample on ice in case you find someone I can match it to."

"That's cold," I said. "I mean, what kind of a guy has an orgasm, then immediately plunges a knife into the back of the guy who gave him the pleasure?"

"That's what they pay you to find out, isn't it? Let me know if you find some semen for me to match."

I hung up with Doc and I walked to my boss's office. Lieutenant Sampson was a big, burly guy fond of polo shirts; that day's was a bright ruby red. "I've made some progress on the dead nurse," I said. I sat down across from his desk and laid the evidence out for him.

"So what do you think happened?" he asked, sitting back in his chair.

"That Bohulano left work at the end of his shift and passed by the construction site. I think he made eye contact with the killer, and the two of them ducked into a deserted corner. After the blow job, the killer stabbed him, then hid his body in the dumpster."

"You might want to show the victim's picture around, see if he was a frequent visitor over there," Sampson said. "That is, if you think you can get anyone to admit it."

"It wasn't necessarily a workman," I said. "Could have been anyone passing on the street. I need to get over there and see how carefully they put away their tools."

Sampson looked at me, and burst out laughing. I could feel my face reddening as he read something unintended into my

Freudian slip.

"The weapon was a wallboard saw, which carpenters use, but if one of them was careless and left it lying around, then anybody could have picked it up."

"Your careless fellow would have to leave a work glove around, too," Sampson said.

"Yeah, there's that. I'll take another look at those interviews I did yesterday."

I've never had really good gaydar—the kind of radar that lets a gay man know that another guy might be interested in a bit of same-sex dalliance. My ability had been improving over the year that I'd been out, but it was nowhere near perfect. None of the men I'd spoken to at the site had set off the signs—a tone of voice, the use of a word, or clothes too formfitting.

My friend Gunter had told me, shortly after I came out, that one of the secrets of gaydar was eye contact. "A straight guy on the street won't lock eyes with you, but a gay guy will," he'd said. Surprisingly to me, that held true. A guy's friendliness wasn't truly an indicator of his sexuality, but it was a big start—especially if that eye contact was followed by a smile, and an appraising glance.

I hadn't gotten that vibe from any of the eight carpenters I'd spoken to the day before. I looked at my watch. It was a little after two; if I hurried, I could talk to each of them again before the end of their shift.

Those discussions, however, proved fruitless (excuse the pun). None was willing to admit he recognized Bohulano, no less that Bohulano had been visiting and servicing men after hours. Promptly at three, all eight packed up their toolboxes and left the site. Only Momoa, who I learned preferred to use only his last name, remained.

"You keep this place pretty tidy, don't you?" I asked.

"I try. It's easier now that the building is enclosed. Bums used to sneak in through the security gate, sleep inside, piss in the corners. Now it's pretty hard to get in."

"But the dumpster's outside the fence."

He nodded. "When we call for a pull, sometimes the company don't come 'til after hours. Easier to leave it outside."

"The guys pretty careful of their tools?" I asked.

Momoa looked at me.

"You recognized that saw yesterday, didn't you?"

He shrugged.

"Come on, Momoa. You work on this site every day. You might not know what it's called, but you know it's a wallboard saw, and you know the guys who use it."

"So what?"

"So do the guys leave their tools laying around when they head out? Any possibility some tramp broke in, stole the saw, and used it?"

His eyes told me he didn't believe that story. "Anybody admit to missing the saw?"

He shook his head.

Driving back to headquarters at the end of the day, I put it all together. If only carpenters used wallboard saws, and no carpenter reported a wallboard saw missing or stolen, then the murderer must have been a carpenter who used his own saw and hadn't reported it was gone.

I supposed I could try for a subpoena for DNA samples from all eight carpenters, and match them up to the dried semen found around Bohulano's mouth. But it would be difficult to convince a judge, and expensive and time-consuming to carry out all those tests.

Should I set up surveillance, figuring out which carpenter stayed at the site after the others had gone? Could I set a trap—figure out a way to offer a blow job to each of them and see who responded? In my mind, I went back over their answers. Three were single, and five were married—not that marriage ruled anyone out. All were strong enough to wield the saw and drive it into Bohulano's back.

While I was grilling chicken and green peppers on my balcony hibachi, I called my mother. My dad had been hospitalized a couple of weeks before with a heart problem, and I had begun to call home more regularly to check on him.

"Now that I have to take care of him, I appreciate how nice those nurses were," she said. "I'm sorry I complained about that one who was cranky with him."

I remembered the patients who had complained about Miguel Bohulano. Suppose one of the carpenters had received one of his specialized treatments? I could cross-reference the complaints against the names of the carpenters and see if I got a match.

"Kimo!" my mother said. "Kimo, you listening to me?"

I came back to earth. "Sorry, Mom. I was thinking about a case. You know how to make Dad cooperate. You've been pushing all of us around forever."

She humphed and said a few things about who pushed who. By the time I hung up we were both laughing, and I was looking forward to going to work the next morning.

But my hunch didn't pay off.  None of the eight carpenters had filed a complaint against Miguel Bohulano.

The phone rang at a few minutes after ten. Bohulano's one credit card had been just been used to make a purchase at the Sears at the Windward Mall in Kaneohe. The card had come up as stolen, and store security had detained the man who tried to use it. I said I'd be right there.

I took the Likelike Highway to the Windward Shore. Trees hemmed in the road as it twisted its way through the Ko'olau Mountains, turning sections into cathedrals of nature. As I drove, I puzzled over this development; how did this stolen card fit into the scenario I had constructed? And why had the credit card turned up so far from the scene of the crime?

I ran into a shower when I came out of the tunnel, but the sky cleared as I descended to the  Y-shaped mall. The sun sparkled across the blacktop, and the air was heavy with humidity. Once I reached the security office and came face to face with the offender, I knew I'd been following a red herring. The guy who'd tried to pass the credit card was barely sixteen—he didn't even have a driver's license.

"Tell the detective what you told me," the guard said.

The kid's name was Bryce Johnson; he lived in Kaneohe and he should have been in English class at Castle High. "I didn't feel like going to school so I came over here," he said. "I was hanging around the mall entrance hoping to bum a cigarette from somebody. I looked down into the bushes and I saw the card. I thought somebody had dropped it."

"Uh-huh," I said. "Why didn't you turn it in?"

He shrugged. "I need a new skateboard. I cracked up my old one, and my mom won't buy me another."

"So you thought Miguel Bohulano would," the guard said.

"The dude dropped his card," Johnson said, as if that explained it. "I didn't think you guys would get onto it so quick."

"The dude didn't drop the card there." I thought Bryce needed a bit of scaring straight. "The dude had the card with him when he was murdered. Where were you Monday afternoon around three o'clock?"

Fear blazed in the boy's eyes. "Monday?" he squeaked, in a voice that was half his normal one. "I was in school Monday."

"Yeah, like you're in school today," I said.

"No, swear to God," he said. "I even had detention. I was there until like four-thirty. You can check with Mrs. Pauahi. She watches us like a hawk."

I wrote down the teacher's name, but I knew the alibi would hold up. And I knew there was no way Bryce Johnson had murdered Miguel Bohulano. The murderer had dropped the card out there, hoping to draw the scent away from himself.

The security guard said the store wouldn't charge Johnson for trying to use the stolen card. "But I catch you trying some stunt like this again, you're going to jail, all right?" he said. "You got me?"

Johnson nodded nervously. "Come on," I said. "I'll drop you at Castle High on my way back to Honolulu."

He sat meekly on the passenger side of my truck, only asking me how the victim had died when I'd turned out of the mall and onto the Kam. "He was on his knees," I said. "He'd just given a blow job to a guy, and the guy stabbed him through the back with a saw."

The kid paled. "That's why you go to school, you know," I said. "So you don't end up on either end of a deal like that— killing somebody, or getting killed."

"My counselor says I can get into the community college if I bring my GPA up to a C," he said.

"Then you should do that." I pulled up in front of Castle High. "And if you need a new skateboard, get a job after school," I called, as he jumped out of the truck.

I watched him go up and enter the building, then headed back to the H1, and Honolulu. I was driving along, working out how I would explain my progress to Lieutenant Sampson when I remembered my conversation with my mother the night before.

Suppose the person whom Bohulano had jerked off hadn't made a fuss. I was sure that for every complaint registered against him, there were probably a few patients who either were too drugged out to know what was going on, or too ashamed to speak up.

Before I had to face my sexuality during the investigation of a case, I thought any same-sex impulses were shameful, to be avoided or ignored, and a lot of men went through that. I had been the recipient of an unsolicited blow job myself once, years before, and because of it I had stepped farther back into the closet.

What if Bohulano had jerked off—or blown—a guy who felt so bad about it that he couldn't report the incident? A guy whose anger festered over time until he saw Miguel Bohulano on the street—and saw his chance for revenge.

When I got back to my desk I found Helen Lau's phone number. "If I give you the names of eight men, would it be possible for you to check if any of them were patients at Queen's while Bohulano was a nurse there?"

"I can't tell you anything specific about the patients, you understand, but I think I can do that under the scope of the subpoena," she said.

I read her the names. "This could take a while," she said. "I'll call you back."

I had to leave the office to help out another detective with a stakeout, and I didn't get back until the end of shift. There was a fax from Helen Lau.

Edward Fujii, one of the eight carpenters, had been a patient at Queen's six months before, after an accident on a job site downtown. He had broken his leg and been in traction for several days. Miguel Bohulano had been his nurse for several shifts during that period.

I remembered Fujii, a slope-shouldered half-Japanese guy in his late twenties. Quiet and brooding, he had given me only monosyllabic answers and been eager to get back to work. He lived in Aiea; it was fifteen minutes up the H3 from there to the Windward Mall. He could have dumped the card there to throw me off the scent.

I went in to see Lieutenant Sampson, who was about to leave. His polo shirt that day was navy blue, and he was standing behind his desk packing up his briefcase.

"Can I talk to you for a sec?"

"Sure, Kimo, come on in. Forgive me if I keep working here, but I've got to be in Kahala by five and I know the traffic's going to be a bear."

I ran the case down for him. "Sounds like you've got it."

"I'll prepare the search warrant for a DNA sample today and have a couple of uniforms pick him up tomorrow before he leaves for work."

He agreed, and I set the wheels in motion. By the time I left, it was already too late for surfing, but I didn't want to go right home. Instead, I stopped at the Rod and Reel Club for a beer at the tail end of happy hour. I was relaxing, sipping my Longboard Lager and scanning the room, when I saw Edward Fujii in a back corner. He had that deer-in-the-headlights look a lot of gay men have the first few times they venture out of the closet. Scared of what will happen if someone comes up to them, but at the same time desperately hoping someone will.

I took my beer and walked over to his table. "I'm not surprised to see you here," I said, sitting down. "This your first time?"

He nodded, but didn't say anything. I remembered from his file he was one of the married ones, and I felt sorry for his wife. "People ask me, sometimes, how long I knew I was gay, and I have to admit I knew when I was a teenager, but I wasn't happy about it, and I liked girls well enough. But eventually something happened to me, and I couldn't deny it anymore." I sipped my beer. "That sound like your story?"

He shrugged. "I guess."

"What was it? The thing that made you realize?"

He looked around uncomfortably, as if he was scanning for a way out. "It was the blow job."

"The one Miguel Bohulano gave you in the hospital?"

He nodded. "I never had one from a guy before. And only once or twice before that, from my wife, before we got married. It wasn't the same."

"Nope, it's not the same at all."

"I didn't know what to do. How could I tell my wife? It turned my world upside down."

"It can do that."

"I couldn't stop thinking about it. It was making me crazy. I wanted—I wanted another one, but I didn't know how to… how to…"

"How to find somebody to give you one?" I said gently.

"I guess." He paused, drank the rest of his beer. "I've been working on that job by the hospital for a couple of weeks, and I kept looking, hoping I would see him coming or going from his shift. And then I did, on Monday. Everybody else had left; I was packing up to go myself. I called him over."

"Did he remember you?"

Fujii nodded. "Yeah. We talked for a couple of minutes, you know, him asking me how I was doing, was my leg all better. I was getting a monster hard-on, and he saw it, and he got down on his knees and opened up my zipper."

I didn't say anything. I knew Fujii had to figure it out for himself.

"After he finished, it didn't feel good at all, not like it had before. It felt bad, really bad. I knew I shouldn't have done it. He shouldn't have made me. I just, I don't know, went crazy. I saw the wallboard saw there, and I picked it up and stabbed him. Only once, you know. I couldn't believe I'd done it."

He started to cry. "It'll be okay," I said. "I'll take you down to the station, you can write up what you told me. The part about going crazy, that's good. This wasn't something you planned, it was spur of the moment. A crime of passion, they call it. The judge'll take all that into account."

I gave Edward Fujii a napkin to dry his eyes, and took him downtown for booking.

Back in my single days, when I was living in Waikiki, I often surfed early on Saturday mornings, then rode my bike out along Diamond Head Road, under the shade of tall banyans with aerial roots dropping down around me in straight lines. I loved to round those curves in the road and see the endless Pacific ahead, sparkling turquoise and aquamarine in the shallow depths and deep, dark blue out to the horizon.

The ride was everything I loved about living in Hawai'i in the space of twenty miles. By the time I'd reach the QuickStop in Kahala, I was ready for a break, a bottle of cold water and a chance to browse through their great selection of the latest surfing magazines.

Every time I went there, it seemed, I saw a man in kelly green pants buying ice. I didn't think it was the same man every time; Kahala was an expensive neighborhood beyond Diamond Head, a place where lots of wealthy haole people lived, the kind who wore brightly-colored pants and gave big parties on terraced yards overlooking Black Point and the miles of blue ocean beyond. People like that, I guessed, were always running out of ice.

One Saturday afternoon I was lounging against the front wall of the store thumbing through a magazine when a white-haired haole man came up to me. He wasn't wearing kelly green pants or buying ice, but he could have been. He was that kind of guy. "Excuse me," he said. "But you're a detective, aren't you?"

I didn't look very professional then, in a pair of bright blue compression shorts and a white tank top that said, "I surfed the Banzai Pipeline and all I got was this lousy t-shirt." But I believed in our motto, to protect and serve, and so I said that I was. "Is there a problem?"

"Can I buy you a cup of coffee?" he said, nodding toward a cafe adjacent to the QuickStop. "It's kind of, well, I don't quite know how to talk about it."

"Sure." I put the magazine I'd been looking at back on the shelf and followed him to the café, where he bought a cup of the rich pure Kona coffee they sold, and a bottle of water for me.

The tables faced out on a local street that led down to Kahala Avenue, which ran by the water. It was lined with hibiscus hedges in red, pink and yellow, and guarded by towering king palms, their fronds flapping in the light breeze. We couldn't see the water from there, but by the absence of anything else on the horizon I could tell the land ended not too far away. "My name is Ralph Kelly," he said, as we sat down.

He was about sixty-five, robust, with slightly reddish skin that could have come from continued exposure to the sun or a mild drinking problem. He wore a light yellow Brooks Brothers polo shirt and a pair of plaid shorts that looked like they'd been bought in the same store.

"Kimo Kanapa'aka," I said, shaking his hand. "How can I help you?"

"My son pointed you out to me when you were on television," he said. "He used you as a kind of example. He's gay, you see. He said if a gay man could be a police detective, then he ought to be able to do what he wanted, too." He looked at me. "I'm not making much sense, am I?"

"Why don't you start with the problem? Then maybe everything else will fall into place."

"My son is missing," Kelly said. "Jonathan Kelly. He's thirty years old, five feet ten, sandy blond hair, thinning on the top." He pointed to his own balding head. "He gets that from me."

"Have you reported this to the police?"

He shook his head. "He's been missing three days now, and my wife and I, we didn't know what to do. Then I saw you here, and it was like a sign. Can you help me?"

"I'm sorry. I'm not very prepared for this. Do you have a pen and some paper?"

"Certainly," he said. "And don't apologize. Obviously I'm

bothering you on your day off." He handed me a pen, and then pulled out his wallet. He found a flier of some kind there, looked at it abstractedly, and handed it to me. I turned it over and wrote down the information he'd given me about his son, along with his name, and his address and phone number.

"You realize this is going to become a police matter. I'm not a private detective. Everything I do goes through the system."

"I understand."

"Tell me about your son."

"He said he knew who you were from Punahou," Kelly said, mentioning the prep school I'd gone to in Honolulu. I was one of its less distinguished alumni; it was the school for the cream of Honolulu's high school crop, as well as the place you go if your family has a lot of money. "I'm sure you didn't know him. He was a few years younger than you are. But boys that age are always looking up to the ones a few years ahead."

I nodded. And waited.

"He was a very normal boy. I know nobody made him—the way he is. He was a good boy, quiet, worked hard, didn't like sports but then, I didn't worry about that. He went to college at Berkeley, good solid choice, lots of boys from the islands go there. After he graduated, he lived in San Francisco for a few years. Perfectly reasonable. We saw him often, sometimes here, sometimes there."

He took a sip of his coffee. "About a year ago he announced that he was gay. The signs had been there, but we didn't want to see them. He's our only son, and my wife and I wanted grandchildren." He paused, as if collecting his thoughts. "Six months ago, I had a heart attack. A pretty bad one. Jonathan gave up his job in San Francisco, he wasn't doing much anyway, and came back to look after my business for me. I supply heavy equipment for construction companies."

I wondered if my father had ever hired equipment from Ralph Kelly. Maybe they could get together sometime and compare notes on having gay sons.

I pushed that thought aside and focused on the case. "When Jonathan returned from the mainland, he lived at home?"

Kelly shook his head. "He took an apartment near downtown so he wouldn't have to commute. He did a good job running things, then I got better. I'm afraid we argued a lot."

"Fathers and sons have a tendency to do that."

"Once he stopped pretending, you see, he started showing these…mannerisms, I guess you'd call them. He told me I had to learn to accept him the way he was."

"That's not such a difficult demand," I said gently.

"I know. And for his mother and me, well, we're trying. We went to see that movie, that Birdcage thing. And my wife read a lot about AIDS, you know, to make sure that he was taking care of himself. As for the business, you have to understand, I work in a pretty macho environment. Contractors, laborers, guys who drive heavy equipment. I thought people might avoid doing business with us."

"Did they, while you were sick?"

"Revenues were down, but nobody I've talked to had anything bad to say about Jonathan." He shook his head. "Funny. These macho construction guys, they all seemed to like him. These last couple of days he's been gone, everybody who calls wants to talk to him. They're disappointed it's me."

"Did anything specific happen just before your son disappeared?"

"Nothing really," he said. "I'd been out of the office, as I said, with my heart. I started going in one or two days a week about a month ago, and then Monday I went back to work full time." I could tell from his eyes that he'd made the connection. "Jonathan disappeared on Wednesday."

"Could he have gone back to San Francisco?" I asked gently, allowing Ralph Kelly to make any connections he chose from what he'd figured out.

"I don't know where he'd go."

"Here's what I can do for you. I'll file a report with missing persons, and if you want, I can make a couple of calls."

"My wife and I would very much appreciate that, detective." He stood up. "Again, I apologize for interrupting your Saturday."

I biked back to Waikiki, taking the curves hard and trying not to think about what Jonathan Kelly had done to his father's business that had caused him to run away. The more I thought about it, the more I decided to wait until Monday to institute any formal inquiries. If Ralph Kelly found that his son had been ripping him off, he might want the whole thing hushed up.

By Monday morning, though, I was curious, so I checked the passenger manifests. Sure enough, a passenger named Jonathan Kelly had been ticketed on the Delta red-eye to San Francisco on Wednesday night. Directory assistance for the 415 area code had a number for a J. Kelly on Sanchez Street, a few blocks from Castro Street in the city's most heavily gay neighborhood.

I called Ralph Kelly at his office and gave him the information. "I never considered anything but foul play until you pointed out the connection between my return to the business and Jonathan's disappearance," he said. "I spent most of the weekend here at the office looking over what happened while I was gone."

I had a feeling I knew what was coming, and I felt sorry for all the parties involved.

"We do a lot of our business on a cash basis, you see, small contractors who need to rent a piece of heavy equipment for a few days. They come in, place the order and make a down payment, and then when they return the equipment they pay the balance."

He paused, and I looked around me. A lot of the other cops had kids, and I'd seen the way many of them would do anything to make sure their offspring were safe and happy.

"Our business seemed to be down almost fifty percent while I was out," Kelly continued, "and I assumed it was because I wasn't here to sell. I didn't expect Jonathan to do anything more than keep the doors open. But when I started calling clients they said they'd been renting from me more than ever, that Jonathan had structured a lot of creative deals for them."

"And he took the cash," I said.

"It appears that way."

"I'm sorry, Mr. Kelly."

"It's the way things are. I'm the one who should be sorry, for bothering you."

I told him again that it had been no bother, and then wished him and his wife luck.

\*\*\*

Soon after I came out of the closet, I began teaching a self-defense class for gay and lesbian teens. It wasn't much, but I liked the idea of giving back, and maybe helping some kid have an easier journey than I had.

I got to the Teen Center in Waikiki, housed in the back of an old-style A-frame church, a few minutes early that evening. I stopped in at the office for a chat with Cathy Selkirk, the pretty, diminutive, half-Japanese woman who ran the place.

I found her surrounded by stacks of papers. She'd recently cut her long black hair into a bob, and it always looked crisp and neat even when the rest of her looked exhausted. "What's up?" I asked.

"Grant applications," she said. "I'm trying to get some money to start a GED program for gay teen dropouts." She gestured to the piles of paper. "It's not easy. The school system has already over-allocated its budget for the next school year, and every one of these forms has its own requirements. It's like applying to college all over again."

"How much cash are you talking about?"

"I need ten grand to get the ball rolling," she said. "I've got a teacher lined up and I need a stipend for her and enough to cover the materials. I can't even tell Sandy, because I know she'd want to help, but she already pays most of the bills around here."

Sandy was her partner, a kick-ass attorney. "I've been thinking about getting a part-time job myself to raise some of the money, but if Sandy found out she'd kill me. She already complains that I never write any more."

Cathy was a talented poet with an MFA in creative writing, and I'd read some of her work, published in tiny literary magazines. She grinned and looked down at the papers self-consciously. "I get out of sorts when I don't write."

"Why don't you look for local donors?" I asked. "Ten people to give you a grand each. Even twenty to give you five hundred each?"

"I hate to fundraise," she said. "I'd rather spend ten hours with one of these forms than a half-hour on the phone asking for cash."

I looked at the clock. I heard the chatter of kids out in the hallway and knew they were ready for the next step in self-empowerment. "I'll give it a think," I said.

My kids were a motley group, aged from fourteen to twenty, from limp-wristed pansies to tough little dykes in training. My favorite was a kid named Jimmy Ah Wong, a thin Chinese boy with a bright yellow coxcomb that stood straight up and then, at the very top, drooped over. He looked like a bit actor in a British art film of the 1980s, but he was smart and infinitely kind to the younger kids.

There were sixteen kids waiting for me, Jimmy among them, when I walked into the room. We talked for a few minutes, and then I led them in a couple of warm-up exercises. We did some yoga, to get them in touch with their bodies, and then a couple of simple judo moves, which segued into some basic stuff I'd learned in the police academy about defending yourself and disarming your assailant. Sadly, because of their sexual orientation, they were vulnerable to attack, either at school or on the street.

When we finished, I talked about empowerment, accepting yourself and taking responsibility for your life. The most important thing I thought I could do was to be a role model for them, a strong, self-confident man with a demanding job, who happened to be gay. Even if the confidence part was a big exaggeration most days.

When the class was over they trickled away into the night. I knew that some of them were hookers, and that some snuck back into suburban homes where no one knew their secrets, and I wanted to take every one of them and say, *Someone loves you. Someone will love you in the future. You are all good people.* But there's only so much you can do.

The next afternoon Ralph Kelly called me. "The best I can figure is that Jonathan walked away with about fifty thousand dollars," he said. "Hell, I spent more than that to send him to college. I'm not about to lose my son over some money. Last night his mother and I called him in San Francisco and told him we knew what happened and we didn't care."

"What did he do with the money?"

Kelly paused. I could tell it was difficult for him. "He's got a friend there, in San Francisco. Hell, I don't know, what do you call him? A lover? A partner? I can't keep up with what you're supposed to say. This fellow's sick. He's got AIDS. Jonathan said it was expensive to take care of him, the insurance wasn't covering the drugs. He didn't want to ask us for the money."

"That's a shame," I said. "About his...friend."

"His mother got on the phone then, and asked him if he'd have asked us for the money if the friend was a woman. If they'd been married. Jonathan said, of course. So his mother said, where's the difference? I tell you, sometimes I don't know how lucky I am I married her."

"So you're reconciled?"

"We want them to move here," Kelly said. "I checked, there's a good program at the University, good doctors. We've got a couple of rental properties, Jonathan and his friend could move into one of them, save some money, and Jonathan can come back to work with me. But he won't."

"Why not?"

"There's something wrong. Something's bothering him—scaring him. It's nothing to do with us, or even with the friend, I think. I got the feeling that he was going to tell me about the money anyway, just hadn't had the chance. Something else drove him away." He paused, and I didn't say anything.

Finally he continued. "I wonder if you could fly over to San Francisco and talk to him. I'll pay you, of course, and your expenses. I don't know what else to do."

"I'm not a private detective, Mr. Kelly," I said. "I work for the police force. And this isn't a police matter."

"Name your price," Kelly said. "Ten thousand dollars, if you'll take it. I just want my son back before it's too late—for either of us."

That figure rang a bell. "All right," I said. "I'll take expense money from you, but I want you to write a check for ten thousand dollars to the Gay Teen Center in Waikiki." I explained briefly about the GED program Cathy wanted to start, but Kelly didn't care. He wanted me to go see his son.

I got a red-eye flight Friday night, the same one Jonathan Kelly had taken a week and a half before, and rolled into San Francisco around six-thirty in the morning, tired, bleary and achy. I took a bus service into the Castro, where I'd reserved a room at a bed and breakfast with a country and western theme. It wasn't my taste, but I wanted to be close to Jonathan Kelly and his partner.

The owner, a genial older gay man, didn't have a room ready for me, but he let me take a shower and change into fresh clothes, and after a solid breakfast in a sunny room filled with cowboy wannabes, I was ready to call on Jonathan Kelly. Sanchez Street was narrow and ran parallel to Castro, a few blocks down Market. Tall trees stood on each side, guarding rows of brownstones with steep entrance steps. I climbed one set and rang a bell next to the names Kelly/Kadary.

From shape of the face and the way he carried himself I knew without asking that the man who answered the door was Ralph Kelly's son. I introduced myself and asked if we could talk.

"My father sent you all the way here to talk to me?"

I nodded. "He felt something was bothering you, keeping you from coming back to Hawai'i. He asked me to see if I could help."

"I don't get it. You're a policeman. The gay cop. I read about you."

"If you'll ask me in, I can explain."

"Oh, sure. Sorry." We walked down a narrow hallway to a door that he'd left ajar, and then into a living room with an eight-foot ceiling and big picture windows that looked out to a garden in the back yard. Sitting in an antique wing chair by one of the windows was a man I assumed was his friend, the Kadary of the front buzzer.

"My partner David," he said, by way of introduction. To David, he said, "My father sent this guy to talk to me. All the way from Honolulu."

David Kadary was probably my age, a couple of years older than Jonathan Kelly. He made no move to get up, so I walked over to shake his hand. His grip was strong, and I could tell he had once been muscular and powerful. Now his skin was pale and his head totally shaved. Still, he looked a lot better than many of the AIDS patients I had seen. It was the dawn of new treatments back then, ones that were available to those with the money to pay.

"David's on the new AIDS cocktail," Jonathan said. "His T cells are actually climbing."

"That's good," I said. I sat on a simple wooden sofa that I could tell unfolded to a futon, and Jonathan sat beside me. I told them my story, with Jonathan filling in gaps about my background to David. When I finished, I said, "Your father thinks there's something else wrong. He said he doesn't care about the money, and I believe him."

Jonathan looked at David. His partner nodded, and said, "Go on, tell him."

"I love that work," Jonathan said. "Going out to job sites, bullshitting with the contractors. My father thought I couldn't do it, that I'd be too gay for all those macho guys. But I showed him. I increased bookings nearly twenty-five percent while I was in charge."

"And you pocketed the money," I said.

"For David's medicine. I wouldn't have taken it otherwise." He looked at David, as if for reassurance. "When my father got sick I was stuck. Did I stay here and take care of David, or go there and take care of the business? But David's insurance wouldn't pay for the new drugs, they said they were too experimental."

"Read too expensive," David said.

"I had a shitty job here in the city, selling office furniture. I hated it, but they were pretty flexible about letting me off when David needed me. I knew I couldn't afford the drugs on my salary. So I decided to go home. I sent every penny back here, I swear it."

"Why didn't you ask your parents for the money?"

"I wouldn't let him," David said. "They don't know me. I'm nothing to them. Why should they pay for my drugs?"

"Because you love their son?" I asked, turning to look at him. "Sometimes we're so programmed for our families to reject us that we don't even let them try to accept us. But families have this way of seeing what matters, and they step up to the plate and help you. And sometimes, they even appreciate getting that chance, having you let them in."

I turned back to Jonathan. "I know. When everything fell apart in my life, my parents and my brothers were there for me. I didn't expect them to be, and it wasn't easy for any of them, but they were. And now, more than ever, I know that they love me. Not because they're there when things are good, but because they're there when things are bad, too."

"I joined the Marines when I was seventeen because I had to get away from my folks," David said. "I thought the Marines would make a man out of me. But I did the work all on my own, until now." He pounded the arm of his chair as tears welled up in his eyes. "Damn! I hate this shit!"

I could sense that Jonathan wanted to go to him, but was holding back. In a minute David had control of himself again. "I want to live," he said. "I want to be here with Jonny for as long as I can be. If I have to swallow a little pride, then I'll do it."

"So you'll come back to Honolulu?" I asked Jonathan.

"It's not that easy."

He got up and walked to the big window, looked out at the garden. Both David Kadary and I were silent. It took a couple of minutes before Jonathan turned back to us. "About two weeks ago I made a deal with a Japanese company we'd never worked with before. They had excellent credit references and they were willing to pay well for good equipment. They were working long shifts, see, and they couldn't afford to have machinery break down."

He came back and sat beside me again. "One night I decided to stop by their site on my way home, check things out. My dad did that a lot, go out in the field and see how the equipment's working out. I learned from him that by watching what a client is doing, often you can convince them to upgrade or add equipment. So I drove to this site they have, out near the port. I didn't make a big deal, just parked and walked around. They had rented big halogen lights from us, too, so it was easy to see what was going on."

He hesitated and looked at David, who said, "You've told him this much. Might as well get it all out."

"They were burying these big rusty barrels," he said. "I wrote down the chemical formula on the side, and one of the foremen saw me and started yelling. Suddenly there were these two security goons coming at me. I panicked and ran to my car. I didn't know if they recognized me, or got my license number, but it scared the hell out of me."

He looked at his partner. "I knew that David would tell me to man up. So I did. I called up an old friend in the chemistry department at UH and he told me what the formula was. It's some toxic goop, an offshoot of manufacturing operations."

"Did you tell anybody?"

He shook his head. "I got a phone call early the next morning, as I was getting dressed. This guy, he had some kind of Oriental accent. He told me they knew who I was, where I lived and what I saw. If I told anybody, they'd kill me."

"So you left town in a hurry."

"It was too much, you know?" he asked. "That, and the money I stole from my father, and missing David. I had to get away."

I sat back on the sofa and looked at both of them. "So, now that you've had time to think about things, are you willing to go back? Live in one of those places your parents own, and work for your father?"

"What about these guys? I'll bet they're yakuza or something. They could kill me."

"We stop them," I said. "You point out the place you saw them dumping, and talk to the EPA guys. They can probably keep your name out of it, but they'll need your testimony to get the warrants."

"I don't know," Jonathan said.

"Can you give us a minute?" David said, nodding toward the garden.

"Sure." I stood up and walked out the French doors to the garden. It was sunny but cool back there, maybe low 60's. A stone walkway wove around wildflowers and low shrubs. In one corner a stone bench sat beneath a curved arbor. I sat there and looked up at the sky. I was tired and jet-lagged, and I guess my eyes must have closed.

"We've made a decision." My eyes snapped open and I realized I'd been dozing. I saw Jonathan and David standing in the doorway. It was difficult to tell exactly who was holding who up. "We're going back," Jonathan said.

"We need all the good karma we can get," David said, smiling.

They agreed to let me take them to dinner that night, on Ralph Kelly, and I went back to the bed and breakfast for a short nap. Then I spent the afternoon roaming around San Francisco. Though I'd visited a few times before, I had been in the closet then, and on this trip I had a chance to appreciate the city in all its gay glory.

I browsed my way up one side of Castro Street and back the other, taking short jaunts off onto side streets as well. By the time I was finished I was on psychic overdrive; my senses flooded with drag queens, leathermen, and cute boys in tight shorts and tank tops so close fitting that their erect nipples showed through the fabric. I saw naked guys on greeting cards, calendars, mugs, and virtually any other surface that would take a picture on it. I saw t-shirts with linked male symbols, funny quotes and obscene slogans.

I couldn't help staring at a well-muscled roller blader who zigged and zagged down the middle of Castro Street, shirtless in the 70-degree sun, wearing only a leather strap around his waist and a loose flap of leather in front and in back. His skin was deeply tan, and his black hair was a curly mane that swept down his neck. His features had a vaguely Asiatic cast, indeterminable even to my eye, accustomed to discriminating easily between Filipino and Chinese, Japanese and Hawaiian, Thai and Malaysian.

"Don't even think of going there," a black guy said to me in passing. "I heard he makes these Tarzan yells when he comes."

"Nothing wrong with that," I said, and we shared smiles, and he went on his way.

It was so liberating to be anonymous in a gay culture. It was unsettling that every fag in Honolulu knew that I was the gay cop. Here in San Francisco I was just another guy in a polo shirt and a pair of chinos.

I browsed through new and used bookstores, buying books I knew I could never find in the islands, constantly readjusting my crotch so no one would see how excited I was. But I was sure they knew anyway. I felt like such a rube, but I couldn't help it. I made eye contact a couple of times with cute guys, and every time sent a current that rattled my neurons. By the time I stumbled back to my bed and breakfast I was worn out and yet sexually charged up.

I met Jonathan and David for dinner at an Italian restaurant a block off Castro, where we ate wonderful pasta and talked like friends. David entertained us with some lewd Marine stories, and Jonathan and I traded tales of growing up closeted in a culture that worshipped the naked physique.

"I used to go to the beach to ogle the surfers," Jonathan said. "I was only twelve or thirteen, I didn't know what was going on, but I wanted them to pick me up and carry me out to sea, then come swooping back into shore on their boards with their arms around my waist."

"Once I remember I was all alone in the locker room at Punahou," I said. "I don't remember why, but I'd just come out of the shower and I was naked, and there was this guy, he seemed like an old guy then, but he probably wasn't even thirty, and he had some kid's jockstrap up to his nose and he was smelling it. I think I scared him as much as he scared me, and he dropped the jockstrap and ran out the door."

"And what did you do?" David asked, with a knowing smile.

"I picked it up and smelled it myself," I said. "I got this amazing woody. So I put it on and wore it home under my clothes."

After dinner they took me on a bar crawl. We began at a wooden-floored club that was so crowded we could hardly move, a vast milling crowd drinking from plastic cups and occasionally looking up to video monitors. From there we moved to a couple of non-descript places, dark and half-empty, drinking and laughing.

We ended up at a high-tech dance club, a huge floor lit with swirling neon and a big, U-shaped bar. Across the room I saw the Tarzan I'd seen earlier, now wearing skin-tight compression shorts in bright yellow and a leather vest over his impressively-muscled chest. He had replaced his roller blades with Doc Martens.

David caught me staring. "Go on, he's cute," he said, nudging me. "You're only in town for the weekend. As long as you keep it safe, you've got nothing to lose."

I wasn't quite sure about that. But I looked long enough that Tarzan looked back, and my throat got dry as he moved towards me. There was a predictable reaction in my pants as well. "Hey," he said, as he came up to me. "I'd say we're the two most exotic-looking guys here, wouldn't you?"

I nodded. "That is, unless you come from Iowa, in which case everybody here probably looks pretty damn exotic."

He laughed. We talked for a while, and the sexual tension rose between us. David and Jonathan excused themselves to go home, and eventually my Tarzan, who said his name was Ron, and I did the same.

I'd never done a one-night stand before then, and didn't know what to expect, but the sex was amazing and so was Ron's body. I know, because I explored every inch of it. He didn't yell like Tarzan, but I knew he had a good time. We didn't get to sleep until it was almost daylight.

He woke me around noon Sunday morning, apologizing and saying he had to get to work. I gathered my clothes and noticed the time. "Shit," I said. "I've got to get to the airport." I kissed Ron deeply and then hurried back to the bed and breakfast, where I checked out. I had to take a cab to the airport and barely made it onto the plane before they closed the doors.

Monday morning Ralph Kelly called me at work and told me Jonathan was coming home later in the week, and wanted to meet with me on Friday. By the time we met, I'd gotten more specific details from him and his father about the client who was doing the illegal dumping, and I'd passed the word on to my friend Alex at the EPA. Alex and I met Jonathan and David's plane, and while I took David home to meet the Kellys, Alex and Jonathan went off for debriefing.

My part of the plan worked better than I expected. Ralph Kelly and David Kadary got along well, falling easily into conversation about the Marines, though David's stories were quite different from the erotic ones he had shared with me and Jonathan at dinner. Jonathan's part apparently didn't go quite as well, because when the government driver delivered him to his parents he was pale and nervous.

"What's up?" I asked, pulling him aside.

"They're raiding the site tonight and they want me to point out the specific place I saw them dumping. Kimo, I'm scared shitless." He looked over my shoulder. "I don't want to seem like a wimp. I mean, God, both he and my dad were Marines."

"If you want me to, I'll go with you."

"Would you?" He stood up straighter. "All right." He shook his head, said, "Shit," and then went on into the house to greet his family.

Later that night, we sat in the back seat of a government car, both of us dressed all in black, with black camouflage paint on our faces and black gloves on our hands. "I'm scared, Kimo," Jonathan said. "I'm not as strong as David is. I don't know if I can do this."

"You're plenty strong," I said. "You made it through years of teasing, of lying, of worrying that everything you ever loved or wanted could get pulled away from you if anyone found out the real truth about you. And after all that, you're still a good person. That makes you strong enough in my book."

I took his hand and squeezed. We pulled up about half a mile away from the site, which we could see lit up ahead of us. "They've moved away from the area where you saw the dumping," Alex said when we were out of the car. "We should be able to get in and get our proof pretty easily. Then we call in the troops."

We walked in single file toward the lights, then Alex led us off toward the side. Jonathan walked next to him and they conferred in whispers. We had to climb a low hill, and once Jonathan's foot landed on a loose rock, starting a small slide. He lost his balance and I caught him. I could feel his pulse throbbing in his wrist.

My own was going pretty fast by then, too. Alex and another

agent got shovels, and while Jonathan pointed they began to dig. A third agent and I stood guard. "There! That's the edge of one of the barrels," I heard Jonathan whisper.

Just then I heard movement near me. I turned slowly as a Japanese guy in a security outfit appeared out of the darkness. "Hey!" he said, and from then on, it was all reflex. As I was telling the kids at the teen center, you build up the sense memory in your muscles and let them take over.

I kicked the flashlight from his hand and it went into a crazy spiral, lighting up the sky with a brief flare. Then I had my right hand over his mouth, and with the left I was applying pressure to his neck. He struggled with me for a minute and then crumpled.

"All right," Alex said. "We've got what we need." His radio crackled to life and he gave the orders for the raid. I took Jonathan and we hurried back the way we'd come, leaving the rest up to the big boys.

When we got back to where we'd left the car, there was another one waiting. Dark and blocky, it looked menacing. Jonathan broke from me and ran toward it, and then I saw David Kadary struggling out of the passenger seat. With the door open, I could see Ralph Kelly at the wheel of the car.

~~~

A couple of weeks later I got an invitation to a party at the Teen Center to announce the inauguration of the Jonathan Kelly and David Kadary GED Program for Gay and Lesbian Youth. That Saturday I figured I had enough time for a quick morning surf and then a ride out to Kahala and back.

I was taking a breather at the QuickStop when I saw Jonathan's father, this time wearing those stereotypical kelly green pants and plaid shirt, looking like he'd just stepped off the golf course. In his hands he carried a twenty-pound bag of ice. "For the party later," he said. "You never know when you might need some more ice."

After a long, happy day of swimming, surfing and fishing, capped by a dinner of fresh-caught mahi-mahi, my friend Gunter and I stood in front of the tent we'd pitched at Hookena Beach, the warm ocean breeze caressing our naked bodies. I wondered if this was how my ancestors had felt, standing on a darkened island shore, marveling at the work of the gods: the ocean, the volcanoes, the stars above. Then Gunter grabbed my dick and dragged me into the tent with him.

Back then, before I settled down with Mike Riccardi, Gunter was a friend "with benefits," and we had sex every so often, accidents of circumstance and lust. He was six three, with blond hair shaved down to a spiky buzz. He worked out every day, so that the muscles in his arms and legs were thick and ropy. I was two inches shorter, but regular surfing and swimming kept me in pretty good shape, too. Sex between us was an athletic event, about endurance and the exhilaration of discovering new ways to twist our bodies together, applying pressure and being rewarded with pressure in return.

Inside the tent, we made out for hours, it seemed, holding back our climaxes, kissing, stroking, licking and rubbing in multiple combinations. Time stood still, sped up, slowed down, washed around us in waves. Outside we heard the relentless surf lapping up on the beach, the occasional cry of a shore bird, the creak of wind in the trees.

Gunter took me in his mouth, and I took him in mine, to work each other over the final heights. My body started to hum in a rhythm over which I had no control, and then, something happened. The walls of the tent started to flap, a light breeze grew stronger, and a cool mist floated around us. The tent began to glow with an unearthly green light as Gunter and I climaxed together.

All at once the green glow disappeared and the air grew still.

Gunter and I slumped against each other and he said, "Man, that was some fuck!"

I was baffled and exhilarated at the same time. As a detective, I believed that there was a reason for everything, some cause rooted in human behavior. But I'd had sex with Gunter before, and there had never been any green glow or misty breeze. He was good, but he wasn't that good.

He twisted around and cuddled up next to me, pressing his butt against my tender cock. He took my arm and wrapped it around him, and within moments he was asleep. I lay there, trying to analyze what had happened. I'd seen green glows like that before, in the ocean. Certain fish emitted a phosphorescent chemical, and a big school of them resembled a huge, lustrous wave. Could we have caught a reflection of that?

It might have been a car passing, maybe green neon wired into the chassis. I'd seen those lights around Honolulu. I ran through a half-dozen other possibilities, none of them reasonable, before I shut off my brain, snuggled next to Gunter, and nodded off.

The next morning we were up at sunrise, surfing the incoming tide. For a while, we were surrounded by a herd of pygmy dolphins, and Gunter and I laughed exuberantly as they nosed our boards and our feet, diving and splashing around us, until we dragged our tired, aching bodies back to the tent. I started fiddling with some food while Gunter went inside to change out of his wet suit. He quickly stuck his head back out. "Hey, somebody's been in here," he said. "Come look."

I hurried over. He held the flap up so I could see. Someone had been rummaging in our stuff and spread it out all over the sleeping bag. "Who could have done this?" Gunter asked. "We were always in sight of shore."

I crawled into the tent with him. "What the..." I said, holding up a rubber. Somebody had ripped open the foil wrapper and pulled it out, even stretched it, but it hadn't been used. Gunter had brought a dozen rubbers with him, all the foil packs joined, and someone had taken them apart. "You thought we were going to need all these?"

"You never know," he said. "Ew, look at this." Someone had taken his tube of K-Y jelly and squeezed some of it out, making a nasty little pool on the nylon floor.

"Gunter, you always bring dildos on camping trips?" I asked, holding it up.

They hadn't touched our clothes, or our money, or anything but Gunter's sex toys. "This is weird, man," he said. "I'm not sure I want to stick around here."

"We've already paid for the camping for two nights, and it's too late to pack up and go somewhere else." I put my hand on his crotch and rubbed. "Don't worry, Gunter, I'll take care of you." He frowned, but he stripped off his Speedos and started to clean up.

After lunch, we lounged in the sun, then swam. I wanted to go out for dinner, but Gunter wouldn't stay at the tent by himself and didn't want to leave it alone, so I sent him down the highway. It was funny, this big, muscle-bound guy, who often scared the shit out of men he met in bars, frightened of somebody breaking into our tent and messing with his sex toys. When I heard him return in the rental car, I couldn't resist pulling my rain parka over my head and jumping out of the tent at him, moaning and howling.

It was as if all his tan faded away. "You bastard," he said, when he recovered. "I'll get you."

I let him chase me into the water, where we wrestled, kissed, and groped each other, rolling around on the sand while the gentle surf nibbled us. After dinner we walked up to the park office, where a ranger named Prapakorn Sinthavanuchit was giving a talk about the Big Island and its legends.

He had started a bonfire, and he invited the kids to come up and sit around him. A few were haole and a few were Chinese, but most were mixed race, like me—I have Hawaiian, Japanese and haole grandparents. My friend Harry Ho calls me a Tiger Woods with a bad golf game.

Gunter and I sat with a dozen adults in a large ring behind

the kids, and the shadows of the fire danced across our faces like restless ghosts. Prap began by telling us what a spiritual place the island of Hawai'i was. "We believe the first Polynesian settlers landed here on the Big Island," he said. "This was also the place where they built the first *luakini heiau*." He looked at the kids. "Do any of you know what that was?"

No one answered, so he raised his face to the adults. "Any of you know?"

"It's where they made human sacrifices, isn't it?" I asked.

Prap nodded, "Who knows what *kapu* is?"

One of the Chinese boys raised his hand. "Bad things."

"That's true," Prap said. "At least, they were things the ancient Hawaiians thought were bad. For example, a commoner couldn't stand in the presence of a chief. Women couldn't eat certain foods, like pork and bananas, and they had to prepare their foods separately from food for men. Kapu regulated every aspect of their lives, and the penalty for breaking it was very severe. Do any of you know what that penalty was?"

A little blond boy drew his finger across his neck and made a slicing noise, and everybody laughed. "That's right," Prap said. "Death. There was only one way to avoid it, and that was to come to a place of refuge, like the historic site down the road. How many of you have been there?"

Most people raised their hands. "If you broke a kapu, you had to get to a place of refuge before the chief got hold of you. Once you got the priest to perform a rite of absolution, you'd be okay. But it was hard to get there, and many people didn't make it."

A breeze blew through, stirring the flames and causing sparks to fly as the wood shifted. "There are many stories of people who were killed right before they reached a place of refuge. It's said that their *manas*, or spirits, still remain, just outside the gates, longing for salvation."

The kids started looking around, as if the ghosts were hovering beyond the edge of the firelight. "They say sometimes a spirit will find a live person, and attach to him." Prap smiled. "Haven't you heard about kids who have invisible friends? Maybe they're spirits that can't cross over into the next world." He laughed. "Now let me tell you about Mauna Kea and Mauna Loa and the gods who live inside them."

After an hour the kids looked sleepy and Prap wound down his talk. Gunter and I walked back to our tent, and out of the range of the fire the night was dark and clouds covered most of the stars.

"D'you believe that stuff?" Gunter asked. "About spirits hanging around. The ones that didn't make it into the place of refuge."

I laughed. "You mean ghosts?"

"Well, mana is a pretty powerful thing, don't you think? Doesn't it mean your personal power, the spirit inside you?"

"Yes, but you think that your spirit lives on after you die? And then comes back to mess with somebody's rubbers and dildos?"

"You don't know, Kimo. What if there really is a ghost hanging around? And what if he's attached himself to us?"

"You've got an invisible friend now, Gunter? Wouldn't that make us a threesome?"

He could tell I wasn't believing him so he got quiet. Prap's speech didn't leave either of us in a romantic mood, so we went to sleep, leaving a well-defined space between us. During the night it got cool though, so by morning we were nestled together, Gunter's leg draped over mine and his chest cuddled against my back. We stumbled through a quick breakfast and then went out into the ocean.

The wind turned around noon, making the water choppy and ruining the waves, so we got out, dried off in the sun and thought about what to do next. "I was thinking, maybe we should go over to the Place of Refuge," Gunter said at last.

"I didn't realize you were into that kind of thing."

"Remember, night before last, when we were doing it?" he asked. "Did you notice anything weird?"

"You mean the tent flapping in the wind, and that green light?"

"Exactly! I think that's when the ghost glommed onto us."

"Gunter."

"I'm serious. Then he fooled around with all my sex toys yesterday morning."

"I think that was one of those kids. We just didn't see him."

"Still, Kimo, what if it's true? What if some spirit that couldn't get into the Place of Refuge has attached itself to us?"

"And you think going there will help?"

"Maybe we can take him in there with us."

I looked at Gunter. I had always known him to be firmly rooted in the physical. Very physical, if you counted sex. But we'd never talked about faith, or anything supernatural. "You believe that?"

"I think it's worth a try."

I shrugged. Back in Honolulu, I dealt with strange stuff all the time. I believed in empirical evidence, in cause and effect. But out there on the Big Island, surrounded by weird lava formations and ancient ruins, I was willing to cut Gunter a little slack. "All right." We put on shorts and T-shirts and got into the rental car. Before we took off, I opened all the windows and yelled out, "All aboard for the Place of Refuge." Gunter gave me a look.

We paid our fee and parked in a group of about a dozen cars. "See over there, that stone ruin?" I said. "That's the *heiau*, or temple. But all around it were quarters for kings and warriors. So the only way for a kapu-breaker to get here was by the ocean. You had to face heavy currents and sharks."

We toured around, reading the historical markers, then stopped in front of a group of carved wooden statues called *kii*, said to embody the ancient gods. "There were twenty-three chiefs buried here," Gunter read from one of the markers.

I nodded. "The legend says that their mana remained with

their bones, and they help make this such a powerful place." I moved close to him. "Can you feel it? Feel that power?"

"I feel your dick pressing up against my butt," he said dryly. I looked around and didn't see anyone, so I kissed the back of his neck.

"You know what that does to me, Kimo," he said.

"I know." I reached around to his crotch, and felt him getting hard. "It's doing it."

He turned around so we were facing each other and we kissed deeply, rubbing our dicks together. I ran my hands over his back, and the sun glinted off his golden hair, and I felt a strong sense of peace in my soul. I guess a deeply spiritual place can do that to you.

"So what do you think?" I asked. "Was it enough that we brought your invisible friend here?"

He let go of me, and stepped back. "Now we need to let him go."

"How?"

"Well, you know how he attached himself to us."

"Gunter! There's lots of people here."

"It's a big place. I'll bet we can find some secluded spot."

I wanted to say no, but my body was saying yes. Gunter was determined, and I had to admit that the risk was sexy. We walked up the path until we reached a secluded beach. Since the surf was choppy I didn't think there'd be anyone there, and sure enough, it was deserted. We went inside a small shed to have some privacy.

The shed was rickety, made with ill-fitting boards and a tin roof. Light seeped in through cracks everywhere, but the floor was clean and flat. Gunter stripped off his clothes and laid them down, and I did the same. We stood there, naked and hard, looking at each other.

"It's weird," I said. "I feel like there's someone else here."

"I do too. He's here with us."

"So how do we get rid of him?"

"I don't know. Maybe he wants some fun before he goes." Gunter smiled. I moved over to him and kissed him, and he kissed me back, and soon we were rolling around on the floor, making a mess of the clothes we'd carefully laid out.

It didn't take long before we were both ready to come. There was this great sexual energy between us, more than usual, and when we were close to climax the shed started to creak and that green light appeared again, borne on a cool, damp breeze, and this time it didn't linger, but welled up around us and then burst upwards, collecting around the underside of the tin roof and then, with a big whoosh it was gone, and Gunter and I were spent, clutching each other.

I wasn't sure what had happened. I got up and examined the shaky, ill-fitting boards of the shack. I sniffed the air, got down on my hands and knees to check every inch of the floor. Gunter sat there and watched me.

"You don't believe, do you?" he asked. "That there was a ghost here, and now he's gone. I think this was what he wanted. To get in here, to the place of refuge."

I sat down next to Gunter. "How can you take something like this on faith? What if there's some rational explanation, some chemical in the air, say. Or some kid sneaking around outside, playing, a prank on us?"

"What does it matter? You know, I go over to the AIDS clinic at Queen's Hospital once a week. I read to a guy with CMV, magazines, sometimes the newspaper, sometimes a novel. He's blind, so he doesn't know if I'm reading the right words. Maybe I'm missing a sentence, maybe it's some key to the whole article or the book. But he takes it on faith."

I started to get dressed. I was buttoning my shirt when I turned to Gunter. "You think he was gay? That maybe that's why he glommed onto us?"

Gunter stopped in the middle of pulling on his shorts. "Was being gay a kapu?"

I frowned. "I don't know for sure. But almost anything could be kapu if you did it at the wrong time, or the wrong place, or with the wrong person."

Gunter finished pulling on his shorts, and buttoned them up. He reached over and pushed a few stray hairs up off my forehead. "I kind of miss him," he said. "I hope he's happy now."

We walked back to the car and drove to the campsite. I wasn't sure how I felt, if I believed that we had been visited by a ghost or if I still thought there was some empirical explanation. "I think it's time to get out of here," I said. "If we hurry, we can make it back to Kona and get the last plane to Honolulu."

"I second that," Gunter said. We got out of the car and hurried up to the tent. Gunter went in first, and then stopped so suddenly that I bumped into him and knocked him down, then fell on top of him.

There were two plumeria leis on our open sleeping bags. I didn't even wonder where they'd come from. I knew.

"Do you think..." Gunter asked.

"You know what they call the plumeria, don't you?" Gunter didn't know. "The dead man flower, because you see so many of them in cemeteries. Some of the hula halaus, when they need to make leis for a performance, they go to the cemetery and take the plumerias." Gunter looked at me. "Well, it's cheaper than buying them."

"This is creepy."

I picked up one lei and put it over Gunter's head, draping it around his neck. Then I kissed him once on each cheek. "Go on," I said. "Your turn."

He picked up the remaining lei, put it around my neck, and kissed me. We both wore the leis all the way back to Honolulu.

It was a gray day, the kind the tourist office hates, clouds massing over Waikiki and threatening rain as I drove out to meet Officer Lidia Portuondo and see the body she had found in some rocky scree on the side of Diamond Head. I remember I was listening to the new CD from Brother Iz then, and feeling bummed that he'd died, as I heard his lyric tenor and his plaintive ukulele and realized that there wouldn't be any more music from him.

Lidia was standing in the shade of a broad kukui tree talking with a couple of hikers when I pulled up on Diamond Head Road. Behind her, the land sloped up toward the summit of the extinct volcano, a mix of sparse grass and rocky scree.

She left the hikers as soon as she saw me. "The deceased is a Caucasian male, 45," she read from her notepad. "Photo ID in the wallet identifies him as Barry Pohl, a professor at UH Manoa."

"What made you think this might be a homicide?" I asked. "Could Mr. Pohl have fallen down the trail?"

"Let me show you."

She led me past the hikers, saying to them, "This is Detective Kanapa'aka. He'll want to talk with you as soon as I show him the crime scene."

I nodded to them and followed Lidia up the hill to the spot on the trail where the body lay sprawled face down. Barry Pohl was overweight, dressed in a blue-flowered aloha shirt, jeans, and hiking boots. Blood had congealed around his head, and from the rigor mortis I could tell he'd been dead for some time, perhaps even since the night before.

Lidia and I both squatted next to the body. She used her nightstick to point at his head. "I thought this looked suspicious," she said, and I had to agree. I was no medical examiner, but I had seen my share of dead bodies. If Pohl had simply fallen and hit his head, there would probably be one major bruise. Instead, it looked as if someone had banged his head against the rocky slope over and over again. There were numerous contusions, and a lot of dirt and rock adhered to the wounds. I called for a crime scene team and the medical examiner.

"You're going to make a good detective one day," I told Lidia.

She shook her head. "Not for me. Give me patrol over a desk job any day."

I nodded down toward the hikers. "They found the body?"

"Come on, I'll introduce you."

We walked back down the slope, and I talked to the hikers, a pair of blond college guys from Indiana, out for an early morning exploration of Diamond Head. They hadn't seen anyone around, and had called the police immediately from a cell phone, waiting by the body until Lidia arrived.

I took my own photos of the body and the surrounding area and made a few notes. By then the crime scene team was there, and I left Lidia with them. I knew that she'd stay until the ME arrived to retrieve the body because she was seeing Doc Takayama on the sly.

I collected Barry Pohl's ID and headed back to the office to start learning about who he was. The University's human resources department told me he was an associate professor in the computer science department. His next of kin was a brother in San Jose, and I got the number. When I called to give him the news, he said he hadn't been in touch with his brother for a while and didn't know anything about Barry's life.

I was getting ready to drive over to Manoa to see what I could find out about Barry Pohl when Lieutenant Sampson came over to me. "Can you talk to a vic for me, Kimo?" he asked. "I know you're on that homicide out at Diamond Head, but this woman's here now and she needs to see someone."

"Sure. What's up?"

"Says she was attacked by a dog in Kapiolani Park. She seems pretty shaken up."

Angelina Ruiz was about five-six, pretty in a delicate kind of way. From her name I guessed she had some Portuguese background, but her face had something else, a combination of Chinese or Japanese, maybe even some Hawaiian or Malay. She was wearing a tight polyester blouse in a shimmering pink, and a dark red miniskirt. Her lipstick matched her skirt. I wondered what she'd been doing, out walking in Kapiolani Park dressed the way she was, and one idea came to mind. "I'm Detective Kanapa'aka," I said. "Why don't you come back to my desk, and I'll see if I can help you."

She stopped at my desk and looked around. "Is there anywhere more… private?" she asked, almost in a whisper.

"Certainly." I led her to an empty interview room. "Would you like some coffee, maybe a soda?"

She shook her head. I pulled a chair out for her, and she sat down, pulling down the hem of her very short skirt as she did. She didn't seem to have any physical scars, no bruising or bleeding as a result of the dog's attack, but she did seem fragile. "Can you tell me what happened?" I asked.

"I like to walk through the park," she said. "It makes me feel better."

I nodded, and waited.

"This morning, I was walking along Diamond Head Road, and this big dog came running down toward me, from the mountain." She shifted in her chair, crossing her legs and again pulling down her skirt.

"What time was this?"

"About, maybe, eight o'clock?" She looked at me questioningly, as if she wanted me to confirm the time for her.

"Were you on your way to work?" I asked.

She shook her head. "I don't work until the evenings." She must have seen my raised eyebrow, because she said, "I work the night shift at a call center downtown. We do customer service for mainland companies."

I still wondered what she was doing in a red miniskirt in Kapiolani Park at eight in the morning, but I asked, "Can you describe the dog?"

"Brown and black," she said. "Some kind of German shepherd, but mixed in with something else."

"Tell me what happened."

"He came running up to me, not barking or anything, so I wasn't real frightened. I mean, I like dogs. So I put my hand out for him to sniff."

"You know it was a male?"

"I know. He sniffed my hand, and then he jumped up on me. He was a big dog, and he knocked me down on the grass." She stood up and turned around. Craning her head over her shoulder she said, "I probably have grass stains on my skirt, don't I?"

There was barely enough material there to be stained, but I could see some green streaks. "Yes," I said. "What happened next?"

"He was on top of me." She sat down again. "First he licked my face, and then he…" Her hand started trembling and she stopped talking.

"It's okay," I said.

She looked down at her hand, and after a bit the shaking stopped. "He stuck his nose up my skirt," she said. "He started to lick me down there."

It was not turning out to be my day. If only I'd stayed out at Diamond Head, I might not have been back at my desk when Angelina Ruiz came in. I took a deep breath. "I know this is hard," I said, "but could you be more specific?"

"He started licking my vagina," she said. "He had a really long tongue, rough on the underside, and he stuck it in me and licked. I tried to push him away but he was just too strong. He licked me until I had an orgasm."

Lord help me, I thought. This woman believes she was raped by a dog. I wondered if there was a full moon.

"He must have known," she said. "After I was finished he licked my face once, and then he ran away, back toward Diamond Head."

"Thank you for coming in," I said. "This must have been very hard for you."

She nodded.

"Let me get some basic information from you," I said and turned to the laptop we keep in the interview room. I opened a blank incident report form and began to fill it out.

When I had all the relevant information from her, I said, "I'll make some inquiries, see if there have been any other reports like this, if anybody else has had similar encounters. It sounds like the dog lives in the area, maybe someone in the neighborhood will recognize him."

"Thank you so much," she said, putting her hand on mine. She gave me a flirtatious look, and I wondered if she was one of the few citizens of Honolulu who didn't immediately recognize me as the gay cop.

I pulled my hand gently from hers and got an evidence bag and a pair of tweezers from my desk. I removed some golden-colored dog hairs from her skirt then walked Angie Ruiz back to the reception area.

"So you'll let me know what happens?" she asked.

"Absolutely. I'll be in touch."

I put Angie Ruiz on hold temporarily and drove in what had become a light rain to the University of Hawai'i at Manoa to learn more about Barry Pohl. The Computer Science department was in the Pacific Ocean Science and Technology building. The department's secretary was a short, friendly Japanese woman named Christina Kobayashi, and she willingly pulled Pohl's file, including his resume and a list of the articles he'd published in computer science journals. As far as I could tell, he was interested in techniques for collecting and analyzing data.

"Did you know him?" I asked Christina.

She gave me a look. "Of course," she said. "I'm the department administrator. Everybody comes to me for everything."

She reminded me of my cousin Mahealani, who is a foot shorter than any guy in our family but never lets any of us get the upper hand. I sat down in the chair next to her office. "Tell me about Mr. Pohl. A nice guy? Jerk?"

"Jerk," she said without hesitation. "Worse over the last year or so."

"Really? Why?"

She leaned in close to me, and I knew there was some good gossip coming. "He's been seeing this woman from the sociology department," she said. "Kitty Weaver."

The name sounded familiar but I couldn't quite place it. "She's been a bad influence on him?"

She stood up. "Come on, I'll take you to his office." We walked down the hall, turned the corner, and she stopped at a door with a poster that advertised a book called *Strippers Uncovered* by Kitty Weaver. The blonde in the picture was fully clothed, in a low-cut blouse and a skirt only a bit longer than Angie Ruiz's, but her pose around a fireman's pole (I mean the kind they slide down) was anything but G-rated.

Once, late at night, when the men and women of Engine Company 12 were on a call, Mike took me into their station, and we climbed to the second floor and slid down the pole. We were both drunk, and so horny we didn't even go back to my apartment, making out hurriedly in his truck behind the station, scared every minute that the crew would come back but unable to help ourselves.

"You see?" Christina said, pointing at the poster.

"I remember the book," I said. "Didn't she work as a stripper for a while to do the research?"

"So they say," she sniffed. "I'm not sure it was all research."

She unlocked the door and we went into the small office. Pohl's desk was a mess, covered with papers, inter-office envelopes and the rotting peel of an orange. The bookcase beside it was filled with computer texts and reference books. A publicity photo of Kitty Weaver faced out on the eye-level shelf.

"Could Professor Pohl have been working on anything sensitive, anything somebody might kill him for?"

The corner of Christina's lip curled. "I don't think so. He hasn't published anything for a long time, and students complained that he wasn't involved in his classes any more. Even with tenure, a professor has to do some work, you know."

"You think his lack of interest in work was because of Kitty Weaver?"

"I know it was. He was obsessed with her. He used to help her with her research, going to the clubs with her, and somewhere along the way he went off the deep end."

"Do you think someone connected with her could have killed him?"

"I wouldn't be surprised." She sighed. "I guess I have to find someone to take over his classes."

"I'll let you get back to it," I said. "I'm going to walk around a bit."

By then the rain had stopped, the sun had come out, and a startlingly bright rainbow hung over the lush Mānoa valley. I walked around the POST building, getting a feel for Barry Pohl's environment, and then through the center of the campus to Maile Way, to the Social Sciences building and the Sociology department. I'd been there once or twice before; they have programs on crime, law and deviance, concentrating on Hawai'i and the Pacific Rim, and I'd heard a couple of speakers and panels.

The schedule on Kitty Weaver's office door indicated she was in class until two. I hadn't had any lunch, so I found a truck on the street, got myself a sandwich, and sat watching clouds gather again over the Mānoa valley.

I was back at Kitty Weaver's door when she came down the hallway toward me, trailing students behind her. She was a tall, skinny haole with close-cropped blonde hair. She didn't look like a stripper, and she didn't have the fragile beauty of Angie Ruiz or the perky attractiveness of Christina Kobayashi, but she had a sense of self-possession. The aura she gave out was that she was in control, comfortable in her looks. I could see why Barry Pohl had dated her, why her students followed behind her in eager supplication.

I waited across from her door until the last student had left, then stuck my head in her door and introduced myself. "Come on in," she said. "How can I help you?"

The room was somewhat larger than Barry Pohl's office, and overflowing with as many books. They were stacked on the floor in teetering piles, they filled shelves on three walls, they covered her desk and the brown wooden visitor's chair. "Sorry about the mess." She swept the books from the chair to the floor. They knocked into a pile already there, and they all cascaded together over the Navajo rug.

I told her, gently, about Barry Pohl. "I can't say I'm surprised," she said, when I was finished. "Barry was an obsessive man. I have been trying to break up with him for months, but he won't let go."

"Where were you yesterday evening?"

She fished around on her desk for a minute, and pulled out a crumpled flyer on yellow paper, which she handed to me. It advertised a lecture by a sociology professor from the mainland, to be introduced by Kitty Weaver. "I got there around five-fifteen—I was running late because my dog got loose and I was looking for him. I had to give up because I needed to be here on campus."

I nodded.

"The lecture ran from five-thirty to six-thirty. Then a number of the faculty took Dr. Leahy out to dinner in Chinatown, and we were at the restaurant until nearly ten." She looked at me. "When was Barry...killed?"

"Sometime in the early evening," I said. "Do you know anyone else who might have had a motive to kill him?"

She didn't. We talked for a few more minutes, and I left, without much more than I'd known when I started. Walking out of the Social Sciences building, I saw a familiar profile heading toward me on Maile Way. When he saw me, he broke into a run, tackling me with a big bear hug. "Hey, Jimmy," I said, when I got my breath back.

I'd met Jimmy Ah Wong some time before, when he was a confused gay teenager who'd been taken advantage of by an older man, a crook who'd been using Jimmy's father's pack and ship store to transport illicit merchandise. During the investigation, Jimmy had come out to his father, an old-school Chinese man who'd kicked him out of the house. Jimmy had lived on the streets for a while, but eventually I was able to convince my godparents to take him in so he could finish high school.

When I first met him, Jimmy had a blond cockscomb slicked up with gel, like a bad eighties punk rocker. When he lived on the streets, he'd worn tattered shorts and skin-tight T-shirts, and had a row of holes pierced up and down his ears. The Jimmy before me, though, looked like every other college kid—baggy pants, flip-flops, and an old T-shirt for the Rainbows, the name the UH teams used to go by before some homophobic administrator decided that the name was too gay-friendly and changed the teams to the Warriors. "So how's school going?"

"Pretty good," he said. "You here to check up on me?"

"Somebody's got to keep you out of trouble." I had pretty much adopted Jimmy as a kind of younger brother, my own project, and knowing how he'd turned his life around made me feel good.

"Seriously," he said. "Bet you got a case."

We walked over to a low stone wall and as clusters of students walked past us, shouting, throwing Frisbees and blasting music, I told him about Barry Pohl and Kitty Weaver. "That Weaver chick, she's got a regular entourage," Jimmy said. "Kids who follow her around everywhere. Even a couple of serious dudes."

"What do you mean serious?"

"I mean like big serious," he said. "Football players and shit. I heard some story about that boyfriend, like maybe she had these football dudes to protect her."

"You know any football dudes?"

He gave me a shy look.

"Jesus, Jimmy, you're only seventeen," I said. "Save some guys to have sex with in your twenties."

"I don't go after them," he protested. "They come looking for me."

"Yeah, right." Jimmy was a hot kid, I had to admit. He was skinny, but he had deceptively strong arms and legs, and I knew that he worked out a lot. Plus I was pretty sure he'd picked up a wide range of sexual skills during his time on the street, when he'd turned more than a few tricks.

"I did hear one weird thing about Weaver. It's probably shit, but you know…"

"What did you hear?"

He leaned in close to me. "I hear she's got this dog, brah, and the dog, you know, does her. With his tongue."

It was turning out to be one of those days. "It's not as strange as you think, Jimmy. I had a woman come in today to the station, she said the same thing happened to her. Only wasn't her dog."

Jimmy shook his head. "Man, this is a weird world," he said. "Shit, I gotta go. I'm already late for class." He leaned over and kissed me, hard and fast, on the mouth. That was a kiss I would neglect to mention to Mike.

I didn't know where else to go so I drove down to Waikiki and parked on Diamond Head Road. It was sunny again down there, a trade wind blowing the clouds up the mountain, and the park was filled with mothers pushing strollers, elderly power-walkers, a Chinese man practicing tae kwon do.

I walked around the area where Barry Pohl's body had been found but no clues to the murder jumped out at me, and then I kept walking and found myself in the area where Angie Ruiz had been assaulted by the mutant German Shepherd. That's when I realized that both her assault and Barry Pohl's had happened close to each other. Kapiolani Park ran right up against the base of Diamond Head.

Around dusk I gave up. I stopped off at the office to pick up the ME's report on Barry Pohl, and took it back to my apartment. While the pasta was cooking I read the report, but there was little in there that I didn't already know. Barry Pohl had died in the early evening of the day before. Cause of death was a brain hemorrhage set off by multiple contusions. Dozens of fine golden and black hairs, probably from a dog, had been found on his body. They had been sent out for analysis, which I would have in a few days.

The next day was Saturday, and I decided to take my morning run by Diamond Head Road. I knew there was something back there I was missing. On an impulse, I checked the phone book to see where Kitty Weaver lived; her address was on Noela Street, between Diamond Head and the park. That had to mean something, but I didn't know what.

I drove to Diamond Head Road, stretched, then ran as far as Black Point and turned around. I came back to the edge of Kapiolani Park and decided to climb up the trail where the body was found, to see if it took me out by the sociology professor's house.

The trail led out to Noela Street. I didn't remember which house belonged to Kitty Weaver, and since I was only wearing a tank top, a jock strap, skimpy nylon shorts with slits up the side and sneakers and socks, I wasn't dressed for further interrogation. Instead I went back down the trail again.

As I came to the bottom of the trail, I saw a familiar silhouette approaching. I was pretty sure it was Angelina Ruiz, dressed in her hooker chic, coming towards me. I didn't notice the big

German Shepherd mix as it came up behind me.

He leaped onto my back and knocked me to the ground. I heard Angie scream in the background, but I was already winded from the morning run and I couldn't get him off me. He planted his front paws on my back and butted my head with his.

"Basker! No! Basker!"

The dog butted me again, but I was still fighting him. Then, all at once, he was off me. "I'm so sorry," a woman's voice said.

I rolled over and looked up, and saw Kitty Weaver standing over me, one hand on the dog's collar. "He usually jumps on people in fun," she said. "And only people he knows."

I sat up. My head was ringing and a couple of stones had dug into my chest. "Is this your dog, Professor Weaver?" I asked.

"Yes, this is Basker."

"From *The Hound of the Baskervilles*?"

"Yes." She looked pleased.

As I stood, holding one hand to the back of my head, where Basker had banged it against the ground, I had a flash of inspiration. "Did Basker know Barry Pohl?"

She grimaced. "Yes. But Basker has better taste in men. He never liked Barry."

I remembered the fine hairs that the medical examiner had picked off Pohl's body, and the ones I'd gotten from Angie Ruiz's skirt. Did they match?

"Professor, I'm afraid I'm going to have to ask you to bring Basker in for some hair samples."

"Don't be silly. He just jumped on you. You won't learn anything from his hair samples."

"I'm afraid this is about Barry Pohl's murder. Mr. Pohl had some dog hairs on his clothing and we'll need to see if they match Basker."

"You can't do that! I'll speak to my attorney! And besides, Barry knew Basker. He could have gotten those hairs on his clothes a hundred different ways."

"I thought you said you and Mr. Pohl had stopped seeing each other a few weeks ago. It's unlikely the hairs would have remained for so long, in such a concentration."

She hesitated. "All right, I wasn't telling you the whole truth. I had been trying to break up with Barry for a long time, but he kept coming around. He was at my house Thursday—but Basker ran away when I opened the door to let Barry in. Barry didn't come in contact with him at all. And then Barry left, and I couldn't find Basker when I had to leave for the seminar. He didn't come home until yesterday morning."

Angie Ruiz appeared next to me. Kitty Weaver still had Basker by the collar, but seeing Angie, he tried to leap out of her grasp. "That's the dog!" Angie said. "That's the dog that attacked me."

"Don't be ridiculous," Kitty said. "Basker isn't a fighter. He's a lover." She leaned down and rubbed her head against the dog's. "Aren't you, Basker?"

I turned to Angie. "You say this is the dog that attacked you?"

She looked frightened, but said, "Yes. I'm sure it is." She stepped up and took my hand. I didn't want to hold hers, but I didn't want to be rude, so I let her stay close to me.

By then I was willing to bet that the hairs would match. "I'm going to have to call an officer to impound Basker immediately," I said.

Fortunately, I saw Lidia Portuondo pass by in her cruiser, and I flagged her down. As she got out of the patrol car, she gave me a funny look when she saw me holding hands with Angie Ruiz. "I need you to impound this dog. Suspicion of murder, and rape."

Lidia's mouth gaped open, matched by Kitty Weaver and Angie Ruiz. Kitty let go of Basker's collar and in an instant, he was on Lidia, knocking her to the ground as he had done with me, and probably with Angie. But instead of butting Lidia's head to the ground, he kept her immobilized with his front paws and began licking her groin.

Angie screamed and grabbed on to me, and Kitty had to pull Basker off Lidia. As soon as she had the dog under control, I reached into Lidia's car and called for some backup. It was going to take a whole army to get that dog to the station.

"She was Miss Saskatchewan the year she graduated from high school," Russell Quant said. "Second runner-up to Miss Canada. He was an all-province running back."

"*Romeo and Juliet* of the Canadian prairie," I said.

Quant smiled and nodded. "Except in our version of the play, instead of ending up dead, Romeo dumps Juliet and moves to Hawai'i."

"Now why didn't ol' Bill Shakespeare think of that?"

"Too cheery."

"I knew there had to be a reason why you were back here in Honolulu," I said. I had met Quant, a Saskatchewan-based private eye, at the Honolulu airport a year before, when he was waiting for a flight home and tackled a runaway suspect for me. He was a good-looking guy, blondish and a bit stocky, with green eyes and long blond lashes. The kind of guy who loved good food, but knew he had to exercise to maintain his figure.

Since then, we had emailed a few times. He was a former cop whose investigations took him around the world, while I was stuck within the limits of Honolulu District One. I was a bit taller than he was and slimmer, with black hair to his blond, and the epicanthic fold to my eyes that I inherited from the Japanese side of my multi-cultural family. Russell liked to say that all he got from his Ukrainian/Irish ancestors was the love of too much good food and drink.

We were both gay men in macho professions, though, and that had solidified a bond between us. When he called to say he was in town, and wanted to buy me dinner at Alan Wong's restaurant, I didn't think it was a date. Russell had a sweetheart, as I did. Instead, I had the feeling he needed a favor.

We met at the restaurant, an unimpressive second-floor space that belied how good the food was, and over a bottle of wine we caught up on his life and mine. As long as Russell—or his client—was paying, I was going to have a great meal. I ordered Da Bag—steamed clams with *kalua* pig and shiitake mushrooms, served in a big foil bag that looked like old-fashioned Jiffy Pop. When the appetizers arrived, I opened the foil and a cloud of steam rushed out, smelling like salt water and rich spice. I inhaled deeply. Russell leaned in to steal a sniff of his own. I took my time savoring each bite, digging the clams out of their shells, mingling them with the shreds of beef and the savory mushrooms.

Russell's appetizer was a quesadilla made with Chinese barbecued pork and mozzarella cheese, which he attacked with hearty gusto.

"Here's the deal, Kimo," he said, as the waiter took away our dirty plates. "Susan—that's my client—used her pageant scholarships to go to secretarial school, and then went to work for an oil and gas company. Frank got a job selling cars. After a couple of years, Frank left her for Honolulu. A year ago, she lost contact with him."

I sipped my wine as he continued his story. I'd have preferred a beer, but he was paying and he knew his way around a wine list.

"She's engaged now," he continued. "She wants a divorce, but didn't have an address to serve the papers. So she hired me."

"She must have a damn good secretarial job, to pay you to come all the way out here."

"Her fiancé is her boss at the oil company, and he's the one paying the bills. He's one of the richest men in Saskatoon."

I snorted. "Is that a big club?"

"Don't knock it 'til you try it, my friend," he said with a good-natured chuckle. "Saskatoon is a surprisingly cosmopolitan city, the Paris of the Prairies they call it."

"Who's 'they'?" I shot back. "You and your mama?"

"At least our ancestors didn't run around wearing grass."

"Better than gopher pelts."

Only the waiter delivering our entrees brought the volleys to an end. As he served, we eyed each other as adversaries, but the smirks on our faces told the true story.

I looked down at my macadamia nut coconut-crusted lamb chops and Quant's sautéed shrimp and clams with penne pasta. "They serve this kind of food there?" I asked, forking some lamb to my mouth, where my taste buds were delighted.

"You'd be surprised."

"Huh."

We dug into the food, not talking for a while. I didn't get to eat at four-star restaurants like Alan Wong's very often, and I figured that I owed Russell Quant big time. "Let's start from the beginning," I said, taking a break from the amazing food. "How'd you get this case?"

"Susan Shapko came to my office last week," he said. "I did some investigation for her fiancé's company last year. He was happy with my work, and knew I'd been to Hawai'i before."

I nodded. "She try to find her ex by herself before she called you?"

"Yeah. Called his mother, a couple of mutual friends. No luck. She's got a big wedding scheduled for three months, so she needs that divorce."

"And the fiancé?" I asked. "How's he feel about this?"

"His name is Tom Kovalevsky. They all went to high school together—Frank, Susan, and Tom. I got the feeling Tom was waiting for his chance with Susan."

"All these names are what? Polish? Russian?"

"Close. Ukrainian."

"I'm assuming you've been looking," I said. "You can't find this guy?"

He shook his head. "I followed every lead I had. Went to the last place he lived, the last place he worked. No dice. You know, kept to himself, didn't talk about what he did outside of work, that kind of thing."

"And that brings you to me."

Handsome smile. "What can you do to help?"

How could I resist? "What info have you got?"

He pulled a piece of paper out of a leather satchel he had with him. "This is everything I have."

I scanned the sheet. There wasn't much, but somehow Frank Shapko had a US social security number. The leads Quant had followed were marked off, but I thought I might try them myself. It was the least I could do, considering I was about to hit him up for my favorite dessert, the "coconut," *haupia* sorbet in a chocolate shell, embellished with tropical fruits and passion fruit sauce. He went for the chocolate sampler.

After some more idle conversation, and a promise to talk again as soon as I had anything to say, he paid the bill and gave me his cell number, and a picture of Frank Shapko taken just before he left Canada. He was chunkier than Quant, with the same sandy blond hair. Shapko had a jutting chin, though, and a nose that looked like it had been broken and poorly reset.

We shook hands while we waited for the valet to bring my Jeep and his rental. It was a hot, humid night, and traffic on South King Street pulsed past us. The only indication that we weren't in any city on the mainland was the piped-in slack key guitar music, and the single palm tree across from us, swaying in the light breeze.

"I'm glad we had dinner," he said as we warmly clasped hands. "Whether you can help me out or not."

"I'll do what I can."

I was busy with a case for most of the next day, but before clocking out I did some quick searching. No John Does at the morgue matched Shapko's description, but I got a hit when I searched criminal records. Shapko had been picked up three months before for a class C felony, possession of one pound or more of marijuana. The case had been dropped, though, and the address on the record was the same one Quant had tried.

I wrapped up for the day and called Russell Quant. "Want to take a ride?"

"Smooth talker. How can I resist an invitation like that?"

I picked him up at his hotel in Waikiki an hour later and we drove out to Pearl City, where Frank Shapko had been living. "I'm telling you, I went out there yesterday and nobody knew the guy," Quant said.

"No offense, Russell, but you're a haole," I said.

He narrowed his eyes and glared at me, unsure what I meant and not liking the sound of it.

I held up my hands in a defensive gesture and explained. "You're a white guy. Driving a rental car."

"So?"

"So there's no incentive for anyone to talk to you," I said. "I may be able to find something out you couldn't."

He shrugged and looked out the window. "Do your best."

To me, the highway was ordinary, but I guess if you come from someplace in the middle of Canada, palm trees against a background of mountains are pretty spectacular. And they probably didn't have those splashes of wild purple bougainvillea either. We passed through a brief shower near the Aloha Bowl stadium, then turned into sunshine as we reached the Moanalua Road exit.

I was driving slowly, looking for the address Quant had visited the day before. A tourist in a convertible seemed like he was tailgating me, but as we pulled up to the apartment building he passed and zoomed ahead.

I could tell from looking at the place where Frank Shapko had been living that it was a hangout for drug users. It was a two-story building, probably a former motel, and most of the parking spaces were full with beat-up Nissan Sentras and Honda Accords, though it was the middle of a Thursday afternoon. A few of the doors were open, and I heard some Jawaiian music beating out of one. "Hawaiian reggae," I said, as we got out of my Jeep. I sniffed the air. "Smell that?"

"Smells the same back in Saskatoon," Quant said.

We followed our noses to an open door on the first floor. I knocked and said, "Howzit, brah?" to the young Hawaiian guy sitting on the bed inside.

He looked at me with red-rimmed eyes. "You know where Frank Shapko stay, brah?" I asked. "Haole guy, blond, Canadian?"

He shrugged. I pulled out my badge and showed him. "Nice pipe you got there, brah," I said, pointing to a big plastic bong on the floor. "Shame for me to have to take it away from you, pull you in for possession, when all I want is to know about Shapko."

"He stay up the mountains, brah." He shrugged. "You know the farmer's market in Kailua?"

"Thursday nights? Like tonight?"

"Yeah, brah. He come down wid a guy sells honey, do his business, then ride back up wid his guy."

"Thanks, brah," I said.

Turning away with Russell Quant, I said, "See, that's how we do it island style."

He shook his head. "Should have taken you to dinner as soon as I got here."

"Well, you'll know better for next time." I looked at my watch. "Market gears up around five. We've got just enough time to make it there before it gets too busy." We drove up the Pali Highway in the light drizzle, with the headlights on and the wipers going, and all the flaps rolled down. Not exactly the picture of Hawai'i we like to show visitors. I noticed Quant was swallowing a lot. "Altitude changes bothering you?" I asked. I pulled a pack of gum from the glove compartment. "Chew this. It'll help."

"We must be climbing pretty high," he said.

"We go through a tunnel in the mountains. When we come out you get a good view of the Windward Coast." It was only late afternoon, but the low cloud cover made it seem like night was coming on fast. We made it into downtown Kailua by four-thirty and parked in the garage behind the Long's. Farmers were already setting up their tables and merchandise, and we found the honey man, a skinny dark-haired haole with a mustache that drooped down at the ends.

"Hey, brah, howzit," I said, showing him my badge.

Quant showed him the picture of Frank Shapko. "You know this guy?"

The honey guy looked from Quant to me. "I just give him a ride, brah. Nothing more."

"That's okay," I said. "You know where he is now?"

He nodded to the right. "He stay down the block. By the shopping center with the taco stand."

Quant and I thanked him, then walked past a clutch of teenagers in front of the Macy's and stopped at the corner. They'd been talking about something as we approached, but shut up as we passed, all eyes watching us. One of them was a kid who came to the gay teen group I mentored in Waikiki, though he avoided catching my eye, and I did the same.

A chunky guy with a deep tan and blond dreadlocks lounged against the front window of the taco stand, talking to a slump-shouldered teenager with torn jeans hanging down his butt. "That your man?" I asked Quant.

"Looks like it." I hung back while Quant approached. The teen took something from Shapko and scurried away, and Quant started talking.

That's when I heard the first gunshot.

"Russell! Get down!" I yelled, as I hit the pavement myself, dropping behind a parked car. There were four shots in all, and the air was still ringing with the sound when I looked up, my Glock in my hand.

Quant was on the ground beside a big SUV; he'd been smart enough to figure out which direction the shots were coming from, and take cover. About a block away, Frank Shapko was racing like he was going for another of those high school touchdowns he was famous for.

One of the bullets had shattered the taco shop's front window, but the others had hit parked cars, without much damage. Quant and I both waited before we moved, then worked our way toward each other, keeping sheltered by cars in the lot. As we met up by a green pickup, I heard an approaching siren.

I used my cell to call in to the Kailua City Police Station to let them know I was on the scene, and when the cruiser pulled up I spoke to the officer, leaving Quant in the background. I explained what I knew, gave him my card, and left him helping the taco store manager call an emergency glass service.

"I didn't even get a chance to introduce myself to him before the shooting started," Quant said. "What was that all about? You think Shapko had somebody watching? They thought I was a cop?"

I shook my head. "I saw the way the shots followed Shapko," I said. "They weren't shooting at you, brah. They were shooting at him."

"At Shapko?"

"That's the way it looked to me. We need to rethink our approach. Come on, there's a good Italian restaurant across the street."

It wasn't Alan Wong's, but it would do. "Can I see a wine list?" Quant asked the waiter. He ordered a 2005 Mazzei Badiola from Tuscany. "You'll like it," Quant said to me, as the waiter left us to look over the menu.

I ordered the artichoke pepperonata, marinated artichoke hearts and roasted peppers, then chicken piccata as my entrée. Quant had the fried calamari and the shrimp scampi. "Can you find out if Shapko's in the middle of some drug problem?" Quant asked. "Somebody who wants to shoot at him to resolve it?"

"My old partner, Akoni, works in Vice," I said. "I'll talk to him tomorrow, see if Shapko's come across his radar."

I thought back to earlier that day, when we'd heard from the stoner that Frank Shapko would be at the farmer's market, and remembered that tourist convertible that had been tailgating me. Had we been followed? Was someone else looking for Shapko, too? Someone who wanted more than his signature on a divorce petition?

I told Quant about the tourist convertible. "The other possibility is that someone's using you to find Shapko," I said. "You notice anyone following you when you were making your rounds?"

Quant thought about that. He was a handsome guy, I reflected, as he did. Too bad we were both in relationships; I would have welcomed the chance to see what he was packing under that conservative striped shirt and khaki pants. But I was in love, and reining in those randy impulses, and I assumed he was, too.

"Now that I think about it," Quant said, "I stopped at a Starbucks this afternoon to pick up an iced coffee, and I didn't want to bother putting the top down on the convertible. I left my briefcase on the front seat while I ran inside, figuring I'd only be gone a couple of minutes. When I got back, the case was still there—but I had the funniest feeling that somebody had turned it sideways while I was inside."

He shrugged. "I worried I was imagining things. But I opened it up and checked my notes. Everything was there—though I hadn't found anything out."

"I'll talk to Akoni tomorrow," I said. "And then I think we should go see our stoner friend again."

I dropped Quant at his hotel and drove the few blocks to my apartment. As I was climbing the stairs, Mike called my cell. "I'm just getting home," I said, walking into my apartment.

"Out late," Mike said. "Big case?"

"More like a favor to a friend," I said. "The guy I had dinner with last night." While I stripped down I told him about my day, and he told me about his. We had dated for a while, then broken up, then started dating again. It looked like the things that had driven us apart the first time were getting better, or at least we were getting a better handle on them.

The next morning, I cleared some time with Lieutenant Sampson, using the shooting the night before as a reason. Even though Kailua was well outside the boundaries of District 1, he was willing to cut me some slack, and I met Quant back at Shapko's apartment building in Pearl City. The stoner's door was closed, and I knocked hard.

No answer.

I knocked again. A twenty-something Hawaiian girl in a sports bra and pajama pants came out of the apartment next door. "You looking for Mickey?" she asked.

"Howzit," I said. "Yeah. He sleep late?"

"He *wen maki*," she said. "Yesterday."

Quant looked baffled. "He died?" I asked the girl. "How?"

"Somebody shoot him." She yawned. "I gotta get ready for school." She went back inside and closed her door.

Quant went to his hotel to make some phone calls, and I returned to headquarters. I spoke to the detective out of District Three who had pulled the case of Mickey's death. He assumed it was a drug deal gone bad, but didn't have any evidence to back that up.

Then I went downstairs to the Scientific Investigation Section and checked with Billy Kim, a skinny Korean ballistics tech I knew. He pulled up both cases and compared the bullets from the shootout in Kailua to the one retrieved from Mickey the stoner.

After a couple of minutes, Billy scooted over so I could look through the microscope. "See the striations on both bullets, where they were marked up as they shot through the barrel? The right-hand twist says that they were both fired from a Smith & Wesson. And those fine little marks at the bottom? Those come from a combination of imperfections in the manufacturing process and wear and tear on the inside of the barrel. That's what tells me they were both fired from the same gun."

I thanked Billy and then left phone messages for the detectives investigating both shootings, letting them know about the ballistics results and that I was looking into the cases based on an ongoing investigation. I left out the part about helping a private eye.

After that I hunted up Akoni. He was a big, beefy Hawaiian who favored XXL aloha shirts. We had gone through the academy at the same time, and then been posted together as detectives in Waikiki, when the department was considering a community policing approach. He was on the phone, but when he finished he said, "Hey, brah, howzit? Don't get you down here in Vice that often."

"Got a question about a doper named Frank Shapko," I said. "Name ring a bell?"

He shrugged, and turned to his computer. "Let me make a call," he said after he'd surfed through a few screens. I thumbed through a pamphlet on drug eradication while he talked to a couple of people, scribbling some directions down on a piece of paper, which he pushed across to me.

"Best I can do," he said. "You go up the Kam and veer off on this side road. My snitch says there's an old trailer up there, and your friend Shapko might be staying there. Supposed to be a *pakalolo* farm somewhere nearby but we haven't found it yet."

"Thanks, brah," I said.

On my way upstairs, I called Quant. "Same gun was used to kill Mickey and to shoot out the taco stand. I've got an address where we can look for Shapko. Maybe he can give us a lead on who killed Mickey while you're getting him to sign his divorce papers."

I picked him up and we drove up the Kam Highway toward the North Shore, keeping an eye out for the local road Akoni's contact had given us. It turned out to be little more than a dirt track, which led up into a heavily forested area. We came to a stream with a narrow footbridge across it. The ground was torn up, indicating that cars had stopped and turned around there.

"You have a weapons permit, back there in Saska-whatchit?" I asked.

"You betya, Kimo Kanapa-whosits," Quant said. "I just don't use it all that often. You sure I need one?"

I unlocked the glove compartment and removed my personal weapon, a Glock 9 mm that was similar to the one the Honolulu PD had issued me. "There's supposed to be a pakalolo plantation around here somewhere," I said. "Let's assume these guys are armed and be as safe as we can."

I gripped the barrel and handed the gun to Quant. I could tell by the way Quant handled it that he knew what he was doing. I pulled my HPD-issued Glock from the thumb holster on my belt and we checked both guns before we got out of the Jeep.

As we walked down to the stream, I sniffed the air, but all I could make out was the smell of trees and mud. Quant crossed the footbridge first, stepping carefully and silently, and I followed. I remembered the way my friends and I had explored the forested tract behind my parents' house when I was a kid and smiled.

We climbed the narrow track, listening to the chirp of birds and the rustle of leaves high above us. When we reached the edge of the woods, instead of pakalolo, we found ourselves at the edge of a plantation. The leaves were narrow and glossy, reflecting bits of sunshine.

"This is not dope," Russell whispered.

"Macadamia nuts," I whispered back. "See the clusters of green nuts at the end of those long stems?"

"Never seen them outside of a box of salted nuts or covered in chocolate."

"Live and learn, brah."

We stayed in the woods, walking around the perimeter of the plantation. After about a quarter of a mile, the trees stopped in front of a ramshackle house trailer, rusted in parts. I wondered how it had gotten so far from the road.

Quant saw Shapko before I did. "Frank Shapko!" he called.

"Russell Quant. I'm a private eye from Saskatoon. I'm not here to arrest you. I only need your signature on some divorce papers for Susan."

Quant and I both trained our guns on Shapko, who looked unarmed. "Susan?" he asked. "She sent you all this way?"

"You're hard to get hold of," Quant said.

"Who's she marrying?" Frank said, and we holstered the guns and walked over to him.

Quant pulled out the paperwork for Shapko. "Tom Kovalevsky," he said.

"No shit? Little nerd? I used to push him around when we were in high school." He crossed his arms. "You know what? I'm not signing. Susan's too good for him."

Quant tossed me his paperwork, and then pushed Frank Shapko up against the wall of the rusty trailer, one arm across Frank's neck. "You don't get to choose who she marries after you, asswipe," Quant said. "Sign the fucking papers."

He nodded to me, and I stepped up with the paperwork and a pen. While Quant kept him immobilized, Frank signed in all the right places. Only then did Quant release him.

"You talk your funny talk and shoot off your guns," Quant said to me with a wink, "This is the way we do it in Saskatchewan."

Shapko stood in front of his trailer, massaging his neck. "You know a doper named Mickey?" I asked him. "Lives in the building where you used to?"

"Yeah, I know Mickey. He's a good guy."

"He's dead."

"No shit?"

"None whatsoever. You got any idea who might have killed him?"

Shapko shrugged. "Nope. He didn't deal, he didn't piss anybody off. Just smoked his dope, worked at his crappy job, and played his video games."

Quant and I began walking back through the woods to my Jeep. "You got your paperwork signed, but we still don't know who killed Mikey," I said. "Or who shot at you and Frank in front of the taco stand."

"I might have an idea," Quant said. He flipped open his cell phone and punched in a number. By the time we got back to the Jeep, he'd finished his call. "You know a hotel called the Kuhio Grande Resort in Kahala?"

"Yeah. Fancy place."

"I was thinking about what Frank said, how he pushed around Tom Kovalevsky when they were in high school," he said. We climbed into the Jeep and I started reversing back down the narrow trail, my hand on the seat back and my head turned to the rear.

Russell Quant looked out the front windshield. "I called Kovalevsky's office and spoke to his secretary. She told me he was at the Kuhio Grande, villa 348."

"You didn't know he was in Honolulu, did you?"

"Nope," he said. "And I don't like clients who use me."

"Don't blame you," I said, as we reached a place where I could turn around. "You want to come with me?"

"Wouldn't miss it."

About a half-hour later, I pulled into the self-parking area at the Kuhio Grande. Quant and I walked through the grounds, checking villa numbers, until we found the right one. I went up to the door and knocked. "Mr. Kovalevsky?" I asked. "Honolulu Police."

I heard voices, someone moving around in the villa, but no one came to the door. "Mr. Kovalevsky?" I said again, louder, and banged harder on the door.

It swung open. A slim, blonde woman in a pink blouse and white tennis skirt stood there. The man next to her, dark-haired and about the same height, had a gun to her head.

"Mrs. Shapko," Quant said. "Mr. Kovalevsky."

"I missed Frank," Kovalevsky said. "But at this range, I guarantee you I won't miss hitting his lousy bitch."

"Tom!" Susan Shapko said. "What's going on?"

"I swore if I ever had the chance, I'd kill your bastard husband," Kovalevsky said. "But then he disappeared. I thought you knew where he was. But you turned out to be as stupid as he was."

"You mean…you don't love me?"

"I wanted you to lead me to Frank," Kovalevsky said.

She twisted around. "You used me! You bastard." She reached up and pounded on his gun arm with her fist, and then kneed him in the balls. He must have already had the safety off, and Susan's reaction caused his finger to slip on the trigger.

By then, though, the gun was pointed at his own chest, rather than at hers, so when it went off his mouth dropped open, and a red splatter bloomed on his brand-new aloha shirt.

Susan Shapko reeled away from him in horror as his blood spattered her pretty pink blouse, and he stumbled to the ground.

I went for the gun, and Quant went for the client. By the time we had both under control, a hotel security guard appeared in response to the sound of the gunshot. Tom Kovalevsky was gasping for breath; it looked like the bullet had entered his heart. Within a minute or two of hitting the ground he was dead.

My partner, Ray Donne, showed up and took witness statements from Quant and Susan, while I handled the medical examiner and the hotel manager, who wasn't happy that there had been a shootout at one of his prime villas. I didn't even notice Quant and Susan leaving.

It was going to take a day for the autopsy, and then another to match Frank's gun to the bullets used in the other shootings. But I arranged to run Russell Quant and Susan Shapko back to the airport the next morning to catch their flight back to Saska-whatchit.

Quant was alone in front of the hotel when I pulled up.

"Where's your client?" I asked, as he loaded his suitcase into the back of the Jeep.

"She's staying here for a while," he said. "I drove her out to Frank's trailer yesterday. They were pretty happy to see each other."

"You going to get paid for all this?" I asked. "What with your client dead and all?"

"Fortunately my contract is with the company," he said, "not with Kovalevsky himself. I think they'll be happy to pay up to make sure this escapade doesn't make the news."

I had to get back to the station, so I only had time for a quick hug as I dropped him off. "Take care, brah," I said. I handed him a box of chocolate-covered macadamia nuts. "A souvenir of your island visit."

He laughed and unzipped the top of his carry-on bag. Inside I could see a stack of boxes, the same brand I'd bought him. "A thank you to Tom Kovalevsky's secretary," he said. "And some motivation for her to push through my invoice."

A few weeks later, I got a FedEx package from Saskatoon. A gift certificate, dinner for two at Alan Wong's. When Mike and I went there to celebrate the anniversary of our first date, I recommended Da Bag and the macadamia-crusted lamb chops.

Ray Donne hung up the phone and turned to me. "You're going to love this one, Kimo," he said. "Somebody stole a hearse with a dead body in it."

"Is it a full moon?" I asked.

"I've got an app on my phone for that. I'll check while you drive."

Ray and I had been working together as homicide detectives in Honolulu District One for a year by then, since his relocation from Philadelphia to the Aloha State. Though we'd had some crazy cases, I couldn't remember anyone stealing a dead body before.

The wind was blowing like a bear as we drove toward the Pali Highway. At least it was coming in from the sea, which meant it was crumbling the waves, and I wasn't missing the chance to be out surfing. The palms along the H1 swayed restlessly, shaking their fronds like manic hula dancers, and stray leaves and fast-food wrappers raced along beside us.

Officer Lidia Portuondo was standing beside her cruiser in the parking lot of a convenience store just off the Pali when we pulled up. She was holding her cap under her arm to keep it from blowing away, and the wind was pulling strands out of her black bun. She introduced us to a middle-aged Japanese man sitting on the sidewalk in front of a big poster for Spam sandwiches. "This is Nelson Okada," she said.

He wore black slacks and a matching polo shirt, with shiny black dress shoes. I stepped forward into the shade of the store's sloping roof and said, "Good afternoon, sir. Can you tell us what happened?"

Okada was holding ice to his head and grimacing. "Somebody stole the goddamn hearse I was driving. Jesus. Who steals a hearse?"

"You work for a funeral home?"

He shook his head, and then groaned. "Body Removal Service," he said. "Funeral homes hire us to move bodies around when they're overbooked."

He didn't have any of the license or registration information on him. "I'm on it," Ray said, and stepped away to call Okada's office.

"Let's step back," I said. "Start with this morning. You show up to work somewhere? Or you get called out?"

"I'm not even supposed to be working today," he said. "My day off. But the boss called me this morning. Had a transport scheduled and the guy who was supposed to do it couldn't. So I went up to the Nuuanu Valley Care Center and picked up a woman who had to catch a flight to the mainland."

"A living woman?"

"I'm not a cab driver, detective. A dead woman."

"So you loaded her in the hearse?"

"Yup. I'm on my way to the airport, driving along behind this panel van, and it was going dead slow," he said. "Then when we came to the stop sign over there, the guy put on his flashers. I was looking behind me to back up when I realized the guy was at my window. I turned to look at him and he knocked me in the head. The next thing I knew I was lying on the sidewalk and the hearse was gone."

A dead palm frond skittered across the parking lot. "Can you ID the man who hit you?" I asked.

"Didn't recognize him. Didn't get a good enough look at him to know him if I saw him again."

"Any details you remember? Haole? Hawaiian? Japanese?"

"Some kind of mix is all I saw," Okada said. "Big guy, dark hair."

That would cover about twenty-five percent of the population.

Ray came back over. "I got the license plate from the office and called in an APB." He looked at Okada. "You were transporting a woman named Florence Evans?"

"That's what I was told," he said. "But the paperwork is in the hearse."

He couldn't tell us much more, so I asked Lidia to take him back to his office, and Ray and I drove up to the Nuuanu Valley Care Center to learn more about Florence Evans.

The heavy wind had knocked down a couple of branches in the parking lot of the V-shaped building. The central section was two stories high, with single-story wings to each side. The grounds could have used a good landscaping—the sparse grass needed trimming, as did the leggy hibiscus hedges.

The receptionist directed us to the office of the administrator, a Filipina named Mercy Suarez.

We introduced ourselves and sat across from her desk. "Can you explain what happened this morning?" I asked

"Our staff nurse pronounced Mrs. Evans dead at seven-forty-five this morning. She was ninety-five and had a history of congestive heart failure, so it wasn't a surprise. Her vitals had been falling for the past twenty-four hours."

I looked at the wall behind her, where a framed diploma from a medical school in the Philippines hung. "You're a doctor yourself?"

"I don't have a license to practice in the US," she said. "So our staff nurse handles everything official."

"Then what?" Ray asked.

"Her next of kin is a niece in San Francisco. She had already made arrangements with Valley Funeral Home, so I called over there. Mr. Robinson said he had another funeral this morning, but he would send someone over to pick up Mrs. Evans."

"That would be Body Removal Service?" I asked.

"Yes. They often come here. We try to be discreet—have them come around to the back entrance. Sometimes they have to wait a while for us to prepare the body, and it's very sad for the other patients to see someone leave in a hearse."

"What can you tell us about Mrs. Evans?"

Mercy shrugged. "She's been here for close to two years. Started as a private pay patient, then her funds ran out about six months ago and she switched over to Medicaid. She couldn't hear well, couldn't see well. Spent most of her time either in bed or propped up in the chair in her room. Nothing special about her—an old woman in failing health who needed care."

Mercy gave us the niece's phone number and took us down a linoleum-floored hallway to the nurse's office. Elaine Connors was a masculine-looking haole with hard-edged features and long, gray-streaked hair. She wore a white lab coat over a low-cut peach blouse that showed the tops of her sagging breasts.

"The aide assigned to her room brought Mrs. Evans her breakfast at seven-thirty and got no response when she tried to wake her. I was paged to her room and checked for vital signs. She was non-responsive, so I pronounced her at seven-forty-five."

"Then what?" I asked.

"I rounded up another aide and a stretcher, and we moved Mrs. Evans out of her room and down to the holding area near the rear exit."

"That's standard procedure?"

I haven't paid much attention to women's breasts since I came out of the closet, but something about the prominent display of hers mesmerized me. I noticed they bounced when she nodded.

"Mrs. Evans was in a three-bed room," Elaine said. "It makes the other patients uncomfortable when the deceased remains in the room for too long."

"Anything unusual about Mrs. Evans or her behavior recently?"

"Not so you'd notice," Elaine said. "As I'm sure Mercy told you, Mrs. Evans suffered from ALS."

"That's Lou Gehrig's Disease?"

Elaine's smile was more of a grimace. "Not that kind. Around here it's an abbreviation for Acute Loss of Sanity. Mrs. Evans was in her own cotton-coated world."

Elaine led us to the room Florence Evans had shared. One of her roommates lay on her side, moaning endlessly, and we couldn't get her to focus on our questions. When the other woman discovered we were detectives she insisted that she wanted to file a complaint about the dog in the house next door, which kept barking all day and all night.

I looked at Elaine. "No house next door, no dog," she said.

We tried a couple of other random patients as we walked toward the front door, with similar results. "Jesus, I hope I never end up in a place like this," Ray muttered.

"At least it's clean. If you call the niece I'll snoop around the building, see if anything looks unusual."

"What are you looking for?"

"I don't know, Ray. Maybe a clue will jump out of the underbrush and bite me on the ass. That would be more than we have now."

"Hey, don't get snippy with me. I was just asking a question." He pulled out his cell phone and I started walking around the exterior of the nursing home. He was right; there was no real reason to look out there, but I had to do something.

Mercy had told us that the second floor was the lock-down unit for Alzheimer's patients; you needed a code to call for the elevator. The right-hand wing was for transient patients who needed rehab after an accident or a fall. There was a small gym at the back of that wing, with a paved patio. As I passed, I saw a therapist encouraging an elderly woman with a walker. Through the big glass windows I saw another therapist with a circle of patients tossing a rubber ball back and forth between them.

The undergrowth often pushed right up against the building's walls, and I had to pick my way carefully. The other wing, where Florence Evans had lived, was for long-term patients, most of them bedridden or needing help with dressing, toileting and other basic activities. I walked past room after room with two or three beds, the curtains drawn open to let in the sunshine.

In the common room at the end of the building, a couple of old ladies were sitting at a table practicing some kind of finger exercises. It looked like they were pushing pills out of blister packs. I guessed that was a good way to save on nursing time, get the old folks to help out with pills.

By the time I rounded the corner to the parking lot I was scratched up, sweating, and even more depressed than I had been before. Ray was finishing his call with Florence Evans' niece.

"Any motive from her?"

Ray shook his head. "She hadn't spoken to her aunt in a couple of years. Mrs. Evans had made her pre-need arrangements before she went into the home—wanted to be buried by her husband in someplace outside San Francisco called Colma."

"I've heard of it," I said. "Most of the city's devoted to cemeteries. Dead people outnumber the living by thousands."

"Lovely," Ray said. "Why would someone steal her body? According to the niece, she was quiet and ordinary. Moved to Honolulu after her husband died, worked as a secretary, retired about fifteen years ago."

"Maybe to cover up the fact that she was murdered?" I suggested. "But it's hard to come up with a motive. She was out of it so she probably didn't piss off anyone else in the home. And according to Mercy, she had run through all her assets."

"Could this be some kind of weird Hawaiian voodoo thing?"

"This isn't Haiti. Zombies don't go around stealing bodies here."

He persisted. "But I've heard about those, what do you call them, night walkers?"

"Night marchers," I said. "If they exist, and I'm not saying they do, they go on foot, to the beat of drums. They don't drive, or steal hearses."

Ray's cell phone rang and he answered. He listened for a minute, then said, "Write this down." He gave me an address near the airport, off the Nimitz. When he snapped the phone shut he said, "Patrol spotted our hearse in a parking lot. Looks like Florence Evans is still inside."

Since there was definitely something suspicious going on, I called Doc Takayama  and asked him to send someone out to pick up Florence Evans' body and give her a good going over.

We got back on the H1 and headed toward the airport. The wind had died down by then but the roadside was still littered with tree branches and bits of black plastic trash bags. Take away the mountains and the palm trees, and we could have been on any highway in the country.

The H1 is elevated around the airport, with the Nimitz huddled below in its shadow. Down there, rental car agencies and airport service businesses cluster, surrounded by acres of parking lots. By the time we found the right one, the ME's van was pulling in. The techs removed Mrs. Evans from the hearse and we gave her a quick look. She was a shrunken woman in her nineties, with iron gray hair. Her face was contorted in a grim rictus of pain and astonishment.

"Not a good way to go," Ray said.

"This look like she died in her sleep to you?" I asked. I've seen a lot of dead bodies—way too many for one lifetime—and Florence Evans looked like she had not gone peaceably to the next world.

"We'll leave that up to the Doc," Ray said.

We called the police impound lot and asked them to tow the hearse in until we figured out what was going on. We arranged to have the hearse dusted for fingerprints while it was there.

It was the end of our shift by then, so I dropped Ray off at headquarters and drove up to the duplex in Aiea I shared with Mike. He was in the backyard grilling a pair of steaks and playing fetch with Roby, our golden retriever. Roby had saved his family from a burning house, but after the destruction of their property they couldn't keep him, so Mike and I had adopted the big goofy dog.

I didn't know how to describe my relationship with Mike in a single word. I already used the term partner for Ray; we spent eight hours a day together, five days a week, and even longer when we were in the middle of a difficult case. Mike and I weren't married, so I wasn't going to call him my husband. He was much more than a boyfriend; we had been living together by then for nearly a year. Although sometimes I wanted to strangle him with my bare hands, he is also the love of my heart and I couldn't imagine life without him.

It was warm, sunny and dry by then, so I stripped down to a pair of board shorts and took over playing with Roby as Mike flipped the steaks and the thick stalks of asparagus on the grill. The food smelled so good, and I thought of Florence Evans, living at the nursing home on a bland diet. Did she have love in her life? Great meals, joy, the love of someone special?

"You're miles away," Mike said, sticking the thermometer fork into a steak. "Bad case?"

"Strange one." I told him about the theft of Florence Evans' body, and my experience at the nursing home. "I'd hate to end up like that, locked away so far from the ocean. You won't let that happen to me, will you?"

"You'll have plenty of people to take care of you," Mike said. "Your brothers, your nieces and nephews. After my parents are gone, all I have is you. And if you go before me? I might end up in one of those places, whether I want to or not."

He stuck the meat thermometer into the thickest part of a steak. "I was reading something the other day," he said. "About health care power of attorney. Gay couples who aren't allowed to make decisions for each other without the right paperwork."

"You think we'd need to worry about that?"

"I think it's time for dinner," Mike said, deflecting the conversation. "These steaks are perfect."

We ate at the picnic table in the backyard, Mike feeding Roby bits of steak under the table, and then after we scraped the grill clean we went inside and watched TV from opposite ends of the big sofa, our legs intertwined, Roby sprawled on the floor. I tried to cherish the moment, because Mike was in and out of burning buildings, and I'd been punched, shot at, and nearly run over in my time on the force.

I had just arrived at headquarters the next morning when I got a call from Charlie Revaldo, the sergeant in charge of the impound lot. "Had a drug dog at the lot this morning to look at a car we brought in," he said. "Dog alerted in front of your hearse. Sat there on his haunches, barking, so I opened up the back door and the dog put his paws up on the platform and sniffed the side, then barked again."

"For what?" I asked.

"You ever see the inside of one of those things?"

"Not yet," I said. "Give me fifty years or so."

"Funny guy," Charlie said. "Inside's all padded to keep the coffin from banging around on the ride. There's a slit in the side of one panel, and the dog sniffed residue of crystal meth there."

"Any idea how fresh?"

"Had to be pretty strong. He alerted from outside the damn hearse."

"Your search of the vehicle find anything else?"

"Yeah. Found a couple of other slits like that in the padding, but no product anywhere."

I thanked him and told him we'd be in touch once we figured out what was going on.

I called down to the Special Investigations Section on the P2 level for the results of the fingerprint search on the hearse. I was told that the vehicle had been wiped clean—not even a print from the driver or any of the other company employees.

The sun was so bright that it hurt my eyes as Ray and I drove to the offices of Body Removal, a nondescript storefront in an industrial neighborhood near the Aloha stadium. A pregnant young Hawaiian woman was at the reception desk, a big calendar on the wall behind her with jobs and drivers marked. We introduced ourselves and she called, "Frank! Police to see you!" through an open door behind her.

A bluff, red-faced haole came to the door. "I'm Frank Napolitano. Can I help you?"

He had a mustache like Mike's, bushy and black, but the resemblance stopped there. He was short and squat, with an open Hawaiian shirt that showed a gold coin on a chain nestled in chest hair.

We followed him into his office—a metal desk with a padded captain's chair behind it, two hard metal chairs across. A calendar from Valley Funeral Home hung on one wall. That was it for decoration.

"We're investigating the theft of your hearse yesterday," I said.

"When can I get it back?" Napolitano asked. "I'm backed up with pickups and deliveries, and I'm already short one driver."

"It's an open investigation," I said. "Tell us about your hiring practices. You do drug screenings?"

Napolitano laughed, a short bark that reminded me of a sea lion's. Or maybe that was just the mustache. "You gotta be kidding," he said. "I got a hard enough time finding drivers willing to work around dead people, because so many of the ethnic groups we got here go nuts about that stuff. I check to make sure they've got a clean license, they can read a map and they can follow instructions."

"What about Nelson Okada?" Ray asked. "Any problems with him?"

"Nelson's a good guy," Napolitano said. "A walking advertisement for AA. I ain't had no problems with him at all." He shook his head. "Now, Tim Grayson, he's a different story."

"Who was he?"

"'Nother driver. Haole from somewhere in the Midwest who washed up here. Bastard was always sniffling, looking kind of spacey. But he worked hard, that is, until he OD'd on ice. Left me up shit creek, too."

Ice was what we called the smokeable form of crystal meth, a real scourge in the islands. "When was that?" I asked.

"Day before yesterday. Keeled over in the john at the gas station down the street, ice pipe in his hand. Cops said he must have gotten hold of some bad shit."

"You have a list of the jobs he handled the last couple of days before he died?" Ray asked.

"Kiki will give it to you." The phone on his desk rang. "We done here?"

"For now," I said. We stood up and he answered the phone.

Kiki stood up and waddled over to the printer as we walked into the office. "This is a list of the jobs Tim did for the last week," she said, handing us the printout.

I noticed that his last pickup had been at the Nuuanu Valley Nursing Home, a body delivered to the Nakamoto Funeral Home in Aiea. Had he picked up the drugs out there? Or somewhere along the way?

There were meth labs all over the island, and it was easy enough to manufacture the stuff. It took a few hours, and anybody who didn't blow up their high school chem lab could usually figure out how to do it. You needed ephedrine, which you could get from over-the-counter cold remedies, back before they started asking a driver's license for a blister pack of pills; red phosphorus, which came from the striking surface of matchbooks; and hydriodic acid, a liquid form of hydrogen iodide.

Ray and I walked out to my Jeep together. "I'll bet you Tim Grayson was using the hearse to transport crystal meth," I said.

"Suppose he was in the middle of a delivery when he OD'd," Ray said. "And the end customer figured out the drugs still had to be in the hearse, and hijacked it."

"Sounds good. But where did he get the stuff? And where was he taking it?"

"Want to go back up to that nursing home and snoop around some more?"

That reminded me of what I'd seen at the nursing home the first time. "Blister packs!" I said, hopping into the driver's seat.

"Care to elaborate?"

"I looked in a window and saw a couple of old women popping blister packs of pills," I said. "I thought at the time they were combining physical therapy with helping out the nursing staff. But what if those blister packs contained pills with cold medicines inside?"

Ray climbed in next to me. "I'll bet you the nursing home could order as much of that stuff as they wanted and nobody would blink an eye."

Instead of driving up to the Nuuanu Valley Nursing Home we went back to headquarters to figure out where the nursing home bought its medications. I got on the phone and tried a couple of pharmacies in the area. The first two were a wash, but when I spoke to Jose Agatep, the manager of the third, Valley Drugs, he acted very hinky.

"I can't reveal any information on my customers without a subpoena," he said.

"In order to get a subpoena, the police have to show a judge reasonable cause for suspicion," I said. "I need to know if the Nuuanu Valley Nursing Home buys from you, and I'll get the subpoena."

"I'm not saying anything."

"All right, sir. But I have to notify you that your failure to provide basic information makes me very suspicious of your pharmacy. The only way I'm going to know if someone from the nursing home makes purchases from you is to request a squad car to sit in your parking lot and check IDs for all your customers."

"You can't do that!"

"Watch me, brah."

He swore at me for a minute or so—nothing all that inventive, just your garden variety aspersions on me, my mother, and my sexual habits. A couple of the things he called me, like cocksucker, were even true.

When he wore himself out he said, "Yeah, they buy from me. But I'm not telling you nothing else without a subpoena."

"Fair enough," I said. "We'll be there as soon as we get the paperwork together. And I might as well tell you if it looks like you've been messing with any of their records, you'll be coming back downtown with us."

He started cursing again, and I hung up. I wrote up a subpoena and had Ray look it over, then we drove it over to Judge Yamanaka's chambers. Once he signed it, Ray drove us back up the Pali Highway to the drugstore, a few blocks from the nursing home.

Jose Agatep was a Filipino so short I could have patted him on the head, but I figured if I did he'd bite me. He led us into his back room, grumbling the whole time, and pulled up the last six months' purchases from the Nuuanu Valley Nursing Home. As you'd expect, they bought a lot of adult diapers, rubber gloves, and over-the-counter analgesics.

The home also bought a big quantity of products containing pseudoephedrine. There were cartons of Sudafed, Mucinex-D, Claritin-D, Actifed, Contac, and Zyrtec-D.

"You didn't think anything was suspicious about this?" I asked Agatep. Sitting there at his computer, with him standing next to me, our faces were almost level.

He shrugged. "It's an old building, they got a lot of mold up there. The old people sneeze a lot."

"Yeah," I said. "Who do you deal with up there?"

"Different people. Sometimes the manager, Mercy. Sometimes the nurse, Elaine."

I printed out the records we needed. "Paper and ink cost money, you know," Agatep grumbled.

"So does a criminal defense," Ray said. "Better get your

pennies lined up."

We sat in Ray's Toyota Highlander and looked at the printouts. "If one of them is selling meth, she's probably making some good money," Ray said.

We went back to headquarters. While he wrote up subpoenas for both women's bank records, I did some additional digging. Elaine Conners owned a small condo about a mile from the nursing home. She had a mortgage and a car loan.

Mercy Suarez owned a condo, too, but hers was in a luxury building in Mānoa, and there was no mortgage recorded. She drove a late-model luxury sedan, too. "I'll bet you Mercy's our suspect," I said.

We completed both subpoenas, though, because you never know until you see the facts, and made our second trip that day over to Judge Yamanaka's chambers.

"Either Mercy or Elaine is manufacturing crystal meth at the nursing home, and using Tim Grayson to sell it." I said as we sat in the judge's waiting room while his secretary took him the subpoenas.

Ray nodded. "And Grayson had a batch in the hearse when he OD'd."

"But who hijacked the hearse? Someone Grayson was going to sell to?"

"Good question," Ray said. The judge's secretary returned with the signed subpoenas, which we drove over to a senior vice president I knew at the Bank of Hawaii headquarters at the First Hawaiian Center on South King Street in downtown Honolulu. Within a few minutes, we had printouts of the activity in both women's accounts.

"It is Mercy Suarez," I said, after a quick glance. She had a hefty balance in both her checking and savings accounts, and a couple of linked CDs as well.

"Suppose Mercy is supplementing her salary with a manufacturing operation," I said, as we left the building. "She hooks up with Tim Grayson for the distribution. Two days ago, Grayson leaves the nursing home with a dead body and the latest batch of meth."

"He samples the merchandise and ODs," Ray said.

I nodded. "But the stuff is still in the hearse. Mercy wants to get her product back, so she waits for the next time that the hearse comes up, follows it until she has the opportunity to hijack it. She searches it, finds the drugs, and abandons the hearse out by the airport."

"But Nelson Okada said a man knocked him out," Ray said.

"So she had an accomplice."

As we were leaving the bank, Doc Takayama called. "You guys give me the most interesting cases," he said. "Your stolen corpse? Murder."

"Murder? How?"

"Come on over and I'll show you."

We drove to the medical examiner's office on Iwilei Road, just off the Nimitz, in a two-story concrete building with a slight roof overhang. The paint on the building is peeling and the landscaping is overgrown—after all, the dead don't vote. The building is between the Salvation Army and a homeless center—something I always thought was an ironic comment, but maybe was intended as an object lesson to those less fortunate. You never know what the city fathers are thinking, after all.

We pulled into the small parking area in the center of the building, and walked in the glass block entrance. The always cheerful receptionist, Alice Kanamura, directed us to Doc's office.

"You've heard of air embolism, right?" he asked, when we walked in. "Somebody injects an air-filled syringe into the victim's vein, and then that air bubble travels through the vein to the lungs. It gets trapped in the capillaries, which are too tiny to let it pass, and blocks blood getting purified by the lungs. The victim starts gasping for air and dies quickly."

"Sounds like something out of a murder mystery," Ray said.

"You need some skill to do this," Doc said. "You've got to be able to give an injection in the right place to hit the vein. And you've got to have the patient immobilized."

"Like an old woman in a nursing home," I said. "Could a nurse do it?"

He nodded. "Or a doctor."

I remembered that Mercy Suarez had a medical degree from the Philippines.

"It's tricky to diagnose an air embolism," Doc continued. "If you open the patient up on the table, the air bubble can simply escape, and there's no trace that anything happened."

"So how'd you figure it out, Doc?" Ray asked.

"When you told me that she had been pronounced of natural causes, I decided to be extra careful—I thought maybe someone had stolen her body to do something to cover up a crime. So I began with X-rays. That's when I spotted the air bubble in her lungs."

He led us over to a wall-mounted light box and flipped it on. "See? Right there," he said, pointing.

"I'll take your word for it," I said.

"Good idea, since I'm the expert," he said. "I dissected the blood vessels under water, so that I could see the air bubbles escaping."

"Like finding a leak in a bicycle tube by putting it under water," Ray said.

"Exactly. I always knew you were the smarter partner, detective."

"Yeah, yeah, you both love each other," I said. "Anything else?"

He turned off the light box and hung a photo there. "Mrs. Evans' forearm," he said. He pointed. "You can see the puncture wound there."

"Any fingerprints on the body?"

He shook his head. "Whoever did it was smart enough to use gloves. Of course, that's common practice in a nursing home anyway."

We left the morgue. "We have two good suspects," I said. "The administrator, Mercy Suarez, who has a medical degree, and Elaine Connors, the nurse."

"Why kill Florence Evans?" Ray asked.

I thought for a minute. "Maybe she was killed in order to get the hearse back up to the nursing home."

"Seems like we have more questions now than when we started," Ray said. "Who makes the drugs? Who killed Mrs. Evans? And who hijacked the hearse?"

"At least now we know the right questions to ask," I said. "But in order to know more, we're going to need a search warrant for that nursing home."

By the time we prepared the warrant and got it signed, and rounded up a couple of uniformed officers to help us, it was five o'clock. We met Mercy in the lobby. "I'm on my way home, detectives," she said. "Can this wait until tomorrow?"

"I'm afraid not," I said. I showed her the warrant, and she unlocked her office for us. I left Ray there and followed Mercy to the small laboratory where they kept medications and performed a few basic procedures. She opened the door for me, and gave me the key to the medication cabinet.

I checked the orders for drugs against what was in the cabinet and what had been dispensed, and came up with a clear discrepancy. After an hour, Ray joined me. "Got it. I have a spreadsheet where she tracks all the drug sales."

"But we don't have her for the murder," I said. "And unless they have hidden closed-circuit cameras I don't see how we're going to pin that on her."

"So we go for what we can get," Ray said. "We take her downtown and interrogate her. Get her to flip on whoever she was manufacturing the drugs for. That's the greater good here, isn't it?"

I wondered if Florence Evans would have felt that way. But she was, after all, an elderly woman with dementia, and when I balanced letting Mercy go free with the potential good of bringing in a major drug distributor and possibly saving countless lives that way, I had to agree with Ray. "But we start with the murder," I said. "Give her a chance to plead down."

We walked out to the lobby together, where Mercy sat with Lidia Portuondo. "Mercy Suarez, you are under arrest for the murder of Florence Evans." I pulled the handcuffs off my belt and as I cuffed her, Ray read her rights.

"This is ridiculous," she said. "Mrs. Evans was an elderly woman with congestive heart failure. No one murdered her."

"Someone stuck a needle in her forearm and pumped air into her veins," I said. "That's murder in my book."

"I want to speak to my attorney."

"You'll be able to call him from downtown," I said.

I sat in the back of the Highlander with her while Ray drove. "You know, we're curious about something," I said. "We've got you manufacturing the crystal meth at the nursing home and we've got you killing Florence Evans. But who hijacked the hearse? That's where all this started, and that's the piece we're still figuring out."

"I have nothing to say." She turned her head and looked out the window at the mist rising over the trees alongside the highway.

"That's your right, of course," I said. "But if you could point us toward a dealer, and as a result we take some of that meth or ice off the street, that could make things easier for you when it comes to charging you. There's a big difference between first-degree murder and manslaughter, you know."

"I wouldn't know," she said.

The sun had set, and headlights around us cast ominous shadows over the Honolulu Watershed Forest Reserve as we drove through it. The streets of downtown were unusually empty, and it felt almost like some kind of holocaust had swept through while we were up in the Nuuanu valley.

Ray drove into the sally port on the ground level of headquarters and we took Mercy inside for booking. We were back up at our desks filling out the paperwork when Rory Yang, the sergeant in charge of the holding cells, called. "Your suspect's attorney is here and they want to talk," he said.

"Be right down."

Rory brought Mercy and her attorney, another Filipino named Rafael Cojuangco Quiblat, into an interview room. "Have a seat," I said. Ray and I sat down across from Mercy and Rafael.

"Hypothetically speaking," Rafael said. "If my client had some information to share about a major drug dealer in Waikīkī, what could that do for her?"

"We don't do hypotheticals," I said. "Either she has some information or not. If she does, we call in an ADA who can make a deal."

"Make the call," Rafael said.

We got lucky and an ADA named Rachel Welliver—a young haole with a pouf of black hair and stiletto heels—was in the building already. She joined us a few minutes later. Ray stood up and offered her his chair.

After we made the introductions, she said, "What have you got for me?"

Rafael leaned in to Mercy and they conferred in Tagalog. "Freddy Akana," he said. "You know the name?"

Freddy was a big dealer in Waikiki, but so far we had been unable to make any accusations stick. He was a slippery guy who kept himself insulated from anything dirty.

"I know it," I said. "But you've got to give us more than his name."

"May we use your laptop, Ms. Welliver?" he asked, nodding toward her briefcase.

She opened the computer and logged into the department network.

"May I?" Mercy asked.

Rachel turned the computer toward her. We watched as Mercy logged into her Bankoh account. "These transfers?" she said, pointing a manicured fingernail at the screen. "They come from Freddy's account. You can trace the account number."

It took a lot more maneuvering. Mercy went back to the holding cell, and we got a further subpoena authorizing us to track the money Mercy had received. It took a couple of days to work things out, because we had to bring Vice into the loop and make sure we weren't compromising any of their cases.

Mercy refused to admit to killing Florence Evans, though we were sure it was her hand that had forced that needle into the elderly woman's arm. Rachel Welliver eventually charged Mercy with a number of drug-related felonies, and she pleaded out to a shortened sentence.

Based on her evidence, we got a warrant to search Freddy Akana's office, behind a garage near Diamond Head Elementary School. We caught a break, and confiscated a lot of ice, as well as some cocaine, some heroin and a lot of pakalolo, island slang for marijuana. There was no way to match the drugs Tim Grayson had taken, so no one was indicted on his death, or in the assault on Nelson Okada and the theft of the hearse.

The subpoena for Freddy Akana's bank records led us to a number of other small manufacturers, and enough evidence to put Freddy in the Halawa Correctional Facility for a good long time. Florence Evans joined her husband in the cemetery in Colma, and Mercy went to the Women's Community Correctional Center in Kailua.

A few weeks after Mercy's trial, Mike and I were sitting at the kitchen table, Roby snoring gently behind our chairs. "I got this paperwork the other day," Mike said, handing me a sheaf of pages. "A living will, and health care power of attorney. I figure we ought to get this stuff out on the table, then put it behind us.

Anything happens to me, I want you to be the one to make the decisions. Not that I don't trust my parents—and I know you'd talk to them, if they're still around when anything happens to me."

I didn't know what to say. I took the papers and glanced through them, at what he'd filled in. "You want to be cremated?" I asked.

He nodded. "If that's okay with you. Live by the fire, die by the fire, you know? And I was thinking maybe if you were cremated, too, whenever, we could have our ashes mixed and then spread out in the ocean."

"I remember this couple I saw years ago, at the Rod and Reel Club," I said. "These two old men, together for like fifty years. They both had to be eighty years old, shuffling along, one hanging on to the other's belt." I smiled and reached for Mike's hand. "That will certainly be us. You and me, together forever."

"I thought she was sleeping," the woman said. "But... oh, my God, Detective." She began crying.

"Call me Kimo. There wasn't anything you could have done," I said, putting my hand on her shoulder.

Her name was Cathy Quinn, and she was a pretty blonde haole in her mid-thirties with a healthy tan and an athletic physique. We were sitting in a small conference room next to the pool at the Waikiki Stars resort, a new property sandwiched in between the big hotels on the *mauka*, or mountain, side of Kalakaua Avenue, the main drag through Waikiki.

Through the floor-to-ceiling glass windows, I could see Ray talking with the medical examiner's team outside, and a couple of beat cops blocking access to the pool area where Cathy Quinn had discovered the body of a dead woman on a lounge chair.

Our victim was a haole woman in her late sixties or early seventies, slim, with an unruly head of fine white hair. About five-six or so, she could have been any of a thousand elderly tourists crossing a visit to Hawai'i off their life list.

One of the hotel maids appeared at the door, bearing a tray with paper cups of coffee from the hotel café. Cathy and I helped ourselves.

I sniffed, and then took a sip. It was pretty good, better than we had back at headquarters, where Ray and I had been going over paperwork when the call had come in from the Waikiki Stars.

"Why don't you start from the beginning and tell me what happened."

Cathy clutched her coffee cup, though she didn't drink. "I got up this morning around six," she said. "I guess my body's still on mainland time. I came down to the pool and saw...that woman...sleeping on a lounge chair at the far end of the pool."

"It's okay," I said gently. "Then what?"

"I started swimming my laps. I did twenty, and then I got out and lay down on a lounge."

"Any idea what time that was?"

"It usually takes me a half hour, so it was probably six-thirty, six-forty-five. The sun was just coming up, and I dried off pretty quickly. Then I went back to my room."

I nodded. "And then?"

"I was on my way out a couple of hours later and I saw her, still on her chair. Her skin was starting to burn. I was worried about her so I tried to wake her." She started to shake. "But she wouldn't wake up."

I put my hand on her shoulder again. "I'm sorry for what you had to go through."

"I screamed, and a guy in a hotel uniform came running. I pointed at the woman and then he took over."

"There's no lifeguard at the pool, is there?"

"No. It's all posted. Swim at your own risk."

"Did you see any hotel employees while you were at the pool?"

She pursed her lips and thought. "No, I don't think so. It was pretty early."

I thanked her and she left, clutching her untouched coffee cup. I walked out to the pool, where the ME's techs were taking the woman away. "Any ID on her?" I asked Ray.

He shook his head. "Just a room key. We'll have to get the front desk to swipe it."

A clutch of vacationers stood at the end of the pool area. A mix of middle-aged haoles, the men in board shorts, the women wearing hibiscus-patterned cover-ups that showed flashes of one-piece bathing suits. A pair of young, hip-looking Japanese with asymmetrical haircuts, probably honeymooners.

Though the crime scene team had already been through the area, Ray and I took opposite sides of the pool area and began a careful search, looking for anything that might be out of place, anything that might be a clue. We found nothing.

We told the uniforms they could let the people back in the pool and went inside. The desk clerk on duty swiped the card for us and told us the key would open room 220. Her name was Mary Longobardi, from Allentown, Pennsylvania. Three rooms were registered to her party, the first of which she occupied by herself. Her son, Leo, his wife Jeanine, and their two sons were in the second room. Her two daughters, Renee and Patricia, were in the third room. They'd all checked in three days before, for a week's stay.

There was no one in her room or the second room registered to the party, but in the third, we roused a petite twenty-something brunette from sleep. "Miss Longobardi?" I asked.

"It's Martone," she said. "Patti Martone. Longobardi's my maiden name."

I introduced myself and Ray. "Can we come in?"

She looked behind her. "The room's kind of a mess. My sister and I were out late last night and we crashed when we got back. Don't know where she is now."

"I'm sorry, but we have some bad news," I said. We stayed in the doorway and told her that her mother had passed away during the night. "When was the last time you saw her?"

"Around eleven. My sister and I were going out to a bar, and Mom was going for a late swim."

That explained Mary Longobardi's presence at the pool. It looked like it was going to be an easy case. She'd probably had a heart attack or stroke after the exertion of swimming, and because she had a single room, no one had missed her.

Patti called her brother and sister on their cell phones, and they both joined us back in the meeting room by the pool where I'd met with Cathy Quinn earlier. With Lidia Portuondo's help, we separated the adults and began taking their statements.

The story was consistent; Mary Longobardi loved to swim,

went to the Allentown Y three times a week at home. They all agreed that Mary had begun a pattern on her first night in the hotel: she'd had a cup of tea, then gone for a quick swim before bed.

"There's one last detail we need to wrap up," I said, speaking to the three siblings. "Since your mother died without a physician present, we need to either speak with her physician to go over what happened to her and see that it matches her condition, or the medical examiner has to perform an autopsy."

"We can tell you what her condition was," Leo Longobardi said. He was big, blustery, red-faced and overweight. His wife, Jeannine, was the kind of skinny, mousy woman you often see matched with a guy like that. "She had a lousy heart. It gave out. End of story."

"And that's what we need her doctor to confirm," I said. "Do you have his name and phone number?"

They all looked at each other. Patti said, "She had a fight with her doctor about a year ago. She never went back."

"Cardiologist? Some other specialist who'd have her records?" I asked.

Nobody spoke. Finally Leo said, "I don't want Ma cut up. It's against our religion."

"We're Catholics, Leo," Patti said. "Nothing's against our religion except eating meat on Fridays during Lent."

The three siblings started to argue. The sister, Renee, had the least to say. I guessed from the dynamics that Leo was the oldest, Patti the baby, and Renee the middle child who tried to keep the peace. After a flood of curses, Leo gave up and told us the family would agree to the autopsy.

At Renee's request, I agreed to see if the medical examiner could schedule the autopsy as quickly as possible, so that the family could take Mary's body home for burial.

We expressed our condolences to the family and went out to the front desk. Because any death could be a homicide until proven otherwise, we got a uniform to tape off Mrs. Longobardi's room until we got the ME's report.

"Most likely the family is making a lot of fuss over nothing," Ray said as we threaded our way through the crowds of tourists and beachgoers, past a guy in a yellow feathered cloak handing out flyers for Hawaiian Heritage jewelry and a flock of Japanese tourists. "The autopsy shows the lady died of heart failure, we close the case, they go home. No need to call anybody names."

"It's the way people are," I said. "This sure knocked the hell out of their vacation."

Doc Takayama called the next day with the results of the autopsy. "Body shows traces of oleander," he said. "I'd say you've got a poisoning on your hands."

"Oleander?" I asked. "The flower?"

"Funnel-shaped, bright yellow or peach-colored," Doc said. "You find them all over the island. They call the seeds lucky nuts sometimes, but they're very unlucky—very poisonous. Eating an oleander seed is like taking a hundred digoxin tablets. The heart gets slower and slower, and then stops."

"You think somebody put an oleander seed in her food?"

"Most likely made a tea out of it."

I remembered what Mary Longobardi's family had said about her habits. "What if she went swimming right after drinking that tea?"

"She might have felt a burning sensation in the mouth, vomiting, diarrhea, or dizziness. Her heartbeat would have been slow or irregular, which would have made her tired. If she didn't do anything, she'd have dozed off and eventually her heart would stop."

I asked Doc to fax us his report, and as soon as I hung up I called the Waikiki Stars to make sure that Mary Longobardi's room was still untouched. She told me that the family had wanted to pack up Mary's belongings but they'd been deflected, and the room key had been changed.

I left Ray at the station preparing a search warrant for the three rooms occupied by the Longobardis, and on my way over to the Waikiki Stars I called my brother Haoa, who runs a landscaping company, and asked him about yellow oleander.

"Nasty plant, brah," he said. "Got to be careful how you handle it." He started to describe the plant to me but he interrupted himself and said, "You want me to come over to the place and see if they've got any?"

"That'd be great."

A half-hour later, I met Haoa, carrying two cups of the good hotel coffee, and we walked the grounds of the Waikiki Stars together, looking for yellow oleander. We found a row of shrubs forming a hedge at a corner of the property where it abutted Kalakaua Avenue. "How can you tell?" I asked. There were no yellow flowers anywhere.

He shrugged. "I know plants," he said.

My cell phone rang. Ray was on his way over with the search warrants. "You go, brah," Haoa said. "I'll see if any of these bushes have been cut lately."

I picked up the new card key for Mary's room and met Ray there. We found a canister of herbal tea next to the coffee maker on top of the bureau, and took it into evidence, along with the mug we assumed she'd used, which had a dried residue in the bottom. I left him with the evidence tech and returned to the yellow oleander hedge, where my brother squatted on the ground, a pair of gardening gloves on his hands.

He pulled a stem forward, and I could see where it had been broken off recently. "The sap's poisonous," Haoa said. "Whoever did this had to be smart enough to wear gloves, or you'd see a rash on the hands."

Haoa used a pair of sharp clippers to cut back on the bush. He dropped the broken branch into an evidence bag that I held open. "Thanks, brah," I said. "You think somebody could squeeze the sap out of this branch and into a cup of tea?"

"Probably." He pointed to a second break on the branch in

the plastic bag. "There was probably a nut there, too. Remember we used to play with these at Ojisan's house?"

"Really?" Our mother's father, a Japanese immigrant who'd been brought to the islands to harvest sugar cane, had lived in a shack up on the North Shore, but he'd died when I was a kid. Haoa, eight years older, and our oldest brother, Lui, remembered him much better than I did.

"Yeah. I remember he had hands like leather. He'd pull the nuts off the tree and throw them to us, but he always told us we couldn't touch the tree ourselves and we couldn't break the nuts open or ever eat them."

He left, and as I walked back to meet Ray I wondered which of Mary Longobardi's family knew about those so-called lucky nuts. I found Leo and Jeannine standing outside their room with Ray.

"You got no right," Leo said to Ray.

"This search warrant gives me the right," Ray said calmly. Ray had been a Philly cop for years before moving to Honolulu, so he was accustomed to dealing with blustering jerks like Leo. "Now, if you don't wait somewhere else, sir, I'll have you removed from the premises."

"Come on, Leo," Jeannine said, tugging at his sleeve. "Let them do their job."

Leo was ready to argue some more, but when he saw that I'd arrived to reinforce Ray he must have realized that resistance was futile. Still grumbling, he stalked away down the hall, his mousy little wife following.

We searched the room, coming up with nothing, until I popped open Leo's Swiss Army knife, a complicated gadget which included a fish scaler, magnifying glass, tweezers, and a dozen other blades of unknown use. The medium-sized blade had traces of a white substance, quite possibly the sap of a yellow oleander.

"Got ya, bastard," Ray said. We bagged up the knife for testing, and after we finished with Leo and Jeannine's room, we moved on to the room shared by Renee and Patti. I have to admit, I'd already convicted Leo in my mind, partly based on the bluster, but we were diligent in searching the sisters' room anyway.

We were in the bathroom, almost ready to call it quits, when I found a scrap of a receipt from Long's Drugs stuck to the side of the wastebasket in the bathroom. Using a pair of tweezers, I peeled it away from the can. Most of the receipt was gone, but what was left clearly showed the purchase of a box of rubber gloves.

I repeated what Haoa had told me about the need to use gloves. We took the oleander branch, the Swiss Army knife, and the receipt from Long's back to the station, where the evidence techs promised us a quick turnaround. I wanted to nail the offending Longobardi before they all left to return to the mainland. In the meantime, we sent two of our biggest, burliest uniforms to the Waikiki Stars to get the fingerprints of all four adults.

While Ray tracked down the surveillance tapes from the Long's Drugs where the gloves had been bought, I called in for credit reports on Mary Longobardi and all her kids, and then filled in our boss, Lieutenant Sampson, on our progress. "Remember, the clock is ticking," he said. "I'd rather not have to extradite a suspect back from Pennsylvania. Too much paperwork."

"You got it, chief," I said. By the time I returned to my desk, the credit reports were in. Jeannine and Leo had first and second mortgages on their house, owed money on both cars, and carried balances on all their credit cards.

Patti Martone had been a computer supervisor for a contracting firm, and apparently had been embezzling from the firm. She had been prosecuted, but the judge had dismissed the case due to procedural errors. Subsequently, she'd lost a civil suit brought by her former employers, and there was a judgment against her for nearly half a million dollars.

Renee, the middle child, was the only one of the siblings in good financial shape. She had a solid job as the manager for a garden center, drove a late-model car that she owned outright, and had a low-rate mortgage on a duplex near her job.

Mary Longobardi's late husband had owned a meat-packing plant, which had been sold upon his death. The proceeds, nearly $5 million, had been invested in a portfolio of stocks, bonds, and CDs. In the five years since his death, the portfolio had nearly doubled.

I had finished with the credit reports when Yuri, the Russian immigrant evidence tech, called me with the results. "It's not oleander on the knife," he said. "It's cocaine."

"What the hell," I said. "You sure?"

"Yup. However, the big blade matches the cut on the branch."

"You gave me a heart attack, Yuri."

"All part of the service."

By then, Ray had looked through seventy-two hours worth of surveillance tape in order to find the one which showed Patti Martone purchasing a box of rubber gloves, along with a dozen postcards, a paperback novel, a box of chocolate-covered macadamia nuts and a hula doll in a grass skirt.

"Hey, get all your vacation shopping done in one place," Ray said.

Our shift had ended a few hours before, and I was tired. We agreed to reconvene the next morning, which still gave us plenty of time before the Longobardis' flight left for the mainland.

It was good to spend time with Mike and Roby. Since I didn't get much time to surf anymore, their love was what kept me grounded.

The next morning, after spending quality time with Roby on the living room floor, and Mike in bed, I felt fresh.

"So, Leo and Patti both had motive," I said. I sat at my desk, across from Ray's. "Leo's knife was used to cut the oleander branch, and Patti bought the gloves."

"And they all knew about Mary's habit of drinking tea before swimming," Ray said. "Either of them could have gotten into her room and doctored her tea."

"So who did it?" I asked.

We sent a bunch of uniforms over to the Waikiki Stars to bring in Leo, Jeannine and Renee Longobardi and Patti Martone, and set them up in separate interview rooms.

Unfortunately, they'd had plenty of time to work out their stories. Leo admitted a cocaine habit, but he said he was in a twelve-step program back in Allentown, and the residue on the knife had to be old. He admitted as well that his family was in financial trouble because of his habit, but that he and Jeannine had started to turn things around.

Patti said that she'd bought the gloves because her mother was having bowel problems, and she'd had to help her clean up a couple of times. "Not the most pleasant task in the world," she said. "Mom asked me not to tell anybody else, because she was embarrassed about it."

We had saved Renee for last, because we were hoping that her brother or sister might have copped to the crime first. As expected, Renee said she didn't know anything about any of it—the cocaine, the uniform, the gloves.

I picked up the cup of lousy coffee I'd poured myself in the break room—much worse than the good stuff we'd gotten at the Waikiki Stars. For some reason I remembered walking around the grounds, holding my coffee, talking to my brother Haoa.

Then it clicked. Haoa was a landscaper, so he knew about plants and toxins. Since Renee Longobardi worked at a nursery in New Jersey, she probably knew that stuff too.

"Can I get you anything to drink?" I asked her. "Coffee? Tea? We've got a great oleander tea, an island special."

"But oleander's poisonous," she said, without thinking.

"You knew that, but you still put it in your mother's tea, didn't you?" I asked.

She crossed her arms over her chest and didn't say anything. I looked at Ray.

"You're the middle child, aren't you?" he asked Renee.

She nodded.

"I know that routine," he said. "I'm in the middle, too. My brother was the first grandchild, and he got spoiled like mad. Then my sister, the baby? She's a little performer. Always singing and dancing. Me, I faded into the woodwork."

"I'll bet you cleaned up after their messes, though," Renee said. "Typical middle child. We're always the peacemaker."

"You got that," Ray said. "Your brother and sister seem to get into a lot of trouble, don't they? Makes it tough for you."

"I tried to convince Mother to help Leo and Patti out, to give them both an advance on their inheritance. She had a lot of money, and she could have paid off Patti's judgment and Leo's mortgages, given them both a chance at a fresh start."

"But she wouldn't?"

Renee shook her head. "She said she was only going to spend her money on things she could enjoy. Like this trip."

"So you sped up the timetable," I said. "I can understand that. I've got two brothers, and I want to look after them, too, even though they're older than I am."

Ray and I sipped our cool coffee and waited.

"Mother was being difficult," Renee said. "I got tired of it. Then she got it into her head to take us all to Hawai'i. It was stupid for her to pay all this money when Leo and Patti are in such trouble. I was complaining about it to one of the guys at the nursery, and he told me to watch out for this bush, called yellow oleander. He said he'd been cutting clippings of plants to bring home, and he got a lousy rash."

She looked very pleased with herself. "I did some research and found out you could poison somebody with it. As soon as we got here, I went looking for the plant. It was so easy to find."

"And then you recruited your brother and sister to help you?" I asked.

She shook her head. "I borrowed Leo's knife and some of the rubber gloves Patti bought, but neither of them knew what I was doing. They wouldn't have agreed anyway. They loved her."

From the emphasis she gave to that word, I wondered if Renee Longobardi loved anyone—even the brother and sister she had worked so hard to protect.

While Renee wrote up her statement, I told Leo, Jeannine and Patti that they were free to go. They didn't leave, though; they waited until after I had handcuffed Renee to lead her downstairs for booking.

Patti confronted her. "You stupid bitch. Didn't you know why Mom was having all those bowel problems? Cancer, Renee. She had about six months left."

"You didn't tell me," Renee said. "Leo, did you know?"

"Sure. That's why we all agreed to come to Hawai'i, even though we'd have rather had the cash. I thought you knew, I thought that's why you organized this whole trip. One last chance to spend some time with Mom."

At trial, Renee Longobardi changed her story, saying that she'd known about her mother's cancer all along, that she'd committed a mercy killing to save her mom all that pain and suffering. The jury believed her—until her brother and sister took the stand against her. In the end, she got twenty years, and Leo and Patti split her share of the inheritance.

As for me, I made a point of seeing my parents at least once a week, keeping up on all their ailments and appointments. I made sure my brothers did, too.

A call from the boss on your way to work on Monday morning is never a good way to start the week. "Jogger found a body at an empty lot off Ahui Street about half an hour ago," Lieutenant Sampson said. "Get Donne and go right over there." He paused for a moment. "Sounds like a bad one."

I called Ray and arranged to meet him at the site, a short road that ran parallel to the cut leading into the Ala Wai Yacht Basin, where Gilligan and the Skipper left for their three-hour tour so many years ago.

There were two police cruisers already on the scene, blue lights flashing. Across an empty lot I saw the back of the Children's Discovery Center, with school buses already pulled up out front disgorging a flow of little keikis on a field trip.

Lidia Portuondo stood next to her patrol car with a twenty-something Asian man in a sweat-soaked tank top, nylon shorts, and expensive-looking running shoes. "This is Wing Bing-Bing," Lidia said, introducing us. "He found the body." She turned to the man and said, "Detective Kanapa'aka."

"Can you tell me what you saw?" I asked.

"I live Kaka'ako," he replied in a heavy Chinese accent, pointing behind us to a row of high-rise condos a few blocks away. "I run here every morning. This morning I run past and I see pile of big plastic trash bag. I think bad people to dump trash here. Then I see foot." He shivered. "I don't do anything more, I just call police."

I thanked him, and made sure Lidia had his contact information. Then I joined another beat cop, Gary Saunders, who was standing guard over a haphazard tumble of black plastic trash bags. The foot Mr. Wing had mentioned was clearly visible sticking out of a hole in the bottom bag. The toenails were painted pink and the heel was callused. The bags were already beginning to smell in the early morning heat.

Ray pulled up in his big SUV and I walked over to meet him. "What have we got?" he asked.

"Slice and dice. Bits and pieces of at least one victim, presumably female, in different bags."

He raised an eyebrow. "Presumably?"

"All I've seen so far is a foot with painted toenails." Ray knew as well as I did that it had been a long time since painted toenails were proof of gender.

While we waited for the crime scene team and the Medical Examiner's van to arrive, I got my digital camera, portable tripod, and an L-shaped measuring scale from my Jeep. I made sure the date and time stamp was on, and with Ray's help I began taking pictures of the scene, beginning with the widest angle. You never know what may show up in the background of a shot. I moved in closer and closer, with Ray positioning the measuring scale to document how close I was.

My abilities with technology had improved considerably once I moved in with Mike, who kept me supplied with hand-me-downs as he upgraded his laptop, tablet, phone, and digital camera. And to think, a few years before I'd hardly been able to turn a computer on.

When I was sure I had all the angles covered, I popped the memory stick from the camera and uploaded the pictures to my netbook computer. I created a new folder on the desktop and put the files in there, as well as blank copies of many of the forms we'd have to fill out.

A steady stream of fishing boats left the marina to head out in search of marlin, tuna and wahoo, rigged with fishing poles and gaffs. A half dozen cattle egrets pecked the barren land near the water's edge, and a huge black frigate bird soared on a thermal around us. When I was a kid, my father told me that the old Hawaiians believed that the appearance of a frigate bird meant someone had died. I guess they were right.

The crime scene van pulled up a few minutes later, and Ray and I stood back and let them look for evidence. The sun was high in the sky by then, and the stink from the bags mixed with the sharp tang of dead fish and the smell of salt water. I watched as the techs tweezed hairs from the ground and picked up other bits of physical evidence.

They opened each bag and inventoried the contents, a grim chore I was happy to leave to them. The result was a collection of body parts that appeared to belong to a large-framed twenty-something woman of at least partial Hawaiian background. Her body had been sawed into large pieces and stuffed into the bags along with shreds of clothing.

Ray yawned. "We keeping you up?" I asked.

"Vinnie's doing a good enough job of that." His wife Julie had given birth two weeks before. Little Vinnie had a big set of lungs and didn't mind using them. "What do you think we have?"

"She was a big girl, so whoever did this had to be stronger than she was."

"Or she could have been doped or drunk."

We hashed out a bunch of choices—lover's quarrel, robbery gone wrong, a drug-related homicide. They were all still ideas, though, because until we knew who she was and how she died we wouldn't be able to formulate any real theories.

When the crime scene guys were finished, the ME's techs loaded the bags up and took them to the morgue. When they were done, Ray and I drove around to the couple of businesses in the area to see if anyone had been around to notice the bags being dropped off, but we had no luck. We kept jumping back into our vehicles to cool off between visits, but we were sweaty and cranky by the time we got to the ME's office, a low-slung off-white building on Iwilei Road.

Alice Kanamura told us that Doc was in the examining room, already at work on our corpse. We dabbed some Vicks Vapo-Rub under our noses and walked in to find that he had removed the body parts from the bags and laid them out on a table.

"You brought me a jigsaw puzzle this morning," he said. "I don't like jigsaws."

"We'll keep that in mind for the future," Ray said.

The body parts had been laid out in a rough sort of order, and we confirmed that the victim was a Hawaiian woman in her late teens or early twenties, nearly six feet tall and close to three hundred pounds. Her skin was pockmarked with acne, and her hair was lank and greasy. She had the start of a mustache on her upper lip.

"Cause of death?" I asked.

"Right now I'm saying evisceration," Doc said. "Most of her internal organs are gone."

"Some kind of ritual killing?" Ray asked.

Doc shrugged. "I'll have more information for you once I finish the autopsy."

"No ID on the body, I assume," I grumbled. "That would be too easy."

"Can't help you with that. But she had a couple of tattoos." He rolled her back so we could see the words "da kine" below the hairline, and then showed us a dolphin on her right ankle.

I snapped pictures of the young woman's face and tattoos and once again moved pictures from the camera to the netbook. Then we drove back to headquarters to try and track our mystery woman down.

"Nowhere near pretty enough to be a prostitute," Ray said, as we left the ME's building. "Clothes and her general personal hygiene don't indicate she had money."

"I don't like the way she was cut up," I said. "I wonder if the killer was trying to make a statement."

"Or couldn't dispose of a body that big all in one piece."

Back at the station, we checked missing persons reports and couldn't find a match. Though I didn't like to use the press, I thought that getting her picture out was the best way of finding someone who'd known her.

I looked through the photos and found the least gruesome

head shot of the girl, which I emailed to Greg Oshiro, a reporter I knew at the *Star-Advertiser*, and asked him to put something in the paper. I did the same thing with my oldest brother, Lui, who managed KVOL, a local TV station. Their motto was "Erupting News All The Time," and they loved anything with a hint of sensation. I was sure that a "help us find out who this dead girl is" appeal would get us something.

There wasn't much else we could do without an ID, so we worked on other cases, slogging through reams of paperwork and making follow-up calls. At home that evening, I watched the KVOL news and saw the girl's photo broadcast with our tip line number.

Mike was away at a fire conference in Kona, so I had full responsibility for Roby and our teenage foster son, Dakota. He was one of the kids who'd come to my gay teen group, and when his mother went to prison, we had taken him in. I wondered, as I often did, at how casually some people tossed away their kids, while others struggled so much to have children.

The next morning, I had an email directing me to a recorded call from the tip line.

"Eh, brah, I t'ink I know da kine girl," a man's voice said. "Her name Alamea, and she work at da kine drugstore on Prospect Street in Papakolea." The operator thanked the man and promised that the information would be passed on to the investigating detectives.

I dialed the drugstore. I identified myself and asked if a girl named Alamea worked there.

"Yeah, but she no come to work today," the man who answered complained.

I described the dead girl, and the man verified that sounded like her. "Got ourselves an ID," I said to Ray, and we drove up to the drugstore to verify the girl's identity and learn more about her.

On the way, Ray pulled into a Kope Bean, our local island-based coffee shop. He pulled up at the drive-through window.

"Gotta have some caffeine to stay awake," he said, while we waited in line. "You want?"

"Might as well. My usual."

He ordered himself a Longboard sized Macadamia Nut Latte, and a raspberry mocha in the same size for me. Then he turned the big SUV uphill to where the drugstore sat, at the foot of Mount Tantalus.

We carried the coffee inside and sipped while we waited for the manager to come out from the back. He was a slim, slight Filipino named Luis. "Yeah, that's her," he said, when we showed him the dead girl's picture. He stepped back and crossed himself.

He led us to the office, where he pulled her original application from a file cabinet, and I copied her full name and address into the file I was building on the netbook.

"What kind of girl was she?" Ray asked while I typed.

Luis shrugged. "Slow. Not like retarded, but always take her longer to get things and do things. She work photo counter most of the time because it was same thing over and over, you know? Take film, scan, ring up."

"She have a boyfriend?"

"Alamea? No way. Not even friendly with other staff."

We established that Alamea had worked her shift on Saturday, but she hadn't shown up Sunday. Luis had called her cell phone and gotten no answer. "Now I think, she look sick on Saturday," he said. "She keep shifting foot to foot, squeezing her lips together like something hurt."

Ray bought a monster-sized pack of dried mixed fruit sprinkled with li hing powder, a spicy treat he had become addicted to, and we drove the few blocks to the first-floor apartment where Alamea lived, in what looked like a converted motel. Ray knocked and we waited. No answer.

He knocked again. We were about to start canvassing the neighbors when the door opened slowly to reveal a huge Hawaiian woman in an extra-wide wheelchair. We showed our badges and

Ray asked, "Does Alamea Kekuahona live here?"

"She my daughter, but she no home."

Ray broke the news to her about Alamea's death. "She always babooze, dat one," the woman said, meaning stupid. "What happen? She walk in front of bus?"

"May we come in, Auntie?" Ray asked. It was awkward talking like that in the doorway.

She backed the chair up and let us into a small, dark living room, partitioned down the middle with a faded floral-print bed sheet hung from the ceiling. A single bedroom to the left, a galley kitchen and a small bathroom. There was only one chair at the table.

Her name was Betty Kekuahona, she said, and Alamea was her younger daughter. The older one had gotten married and moved out years before, and when Alamea turned sixteen, she had rigged up the curtain to give herself some privacy.

Betty's hair was pulled back and twisted into a bun that looked like the face of a small, yappy dog, like a Brussels Griffon or an Affenpinscher. Her forearms were massive and lightly dusted with brown hair.

We put on gloves and searched the small space, but there were no clues as to what had happened to Alamea. "She had a cell phone, right?" I asked.

Betty gave us the number. I pulled out the netbook and added it to the list.

"Any friends?"

"None she talk about. Alamea always too big and stupid to make friends."

We gave her the phone number for the medical examiner's office. "How I gonna bury her?" Betty asked. "I got no money. And I got the diabetes bad. Can't work, got to get my medicine from the free clinic."

I brought up the name and phone number for the department's victim advocate from the netbook. I gave that to Betty. "She can help you out," I said. "We're sorry for your loss, Auntie."

She shrugged. "I always knew dat girl would do something stupid one day."

We got in Ray's SUV and he backed out of the parking space. "Not exactly broken up, is she? That was her daughter."

"Makes me feel bad for Alamea," I said. "Fat, homely, no friends, a boss who thought she was slow and a mother who thought she was stupid."

"Not the kind of person you'd think would end up the way she did," Ray added.

When we got back to headquarters we put together a subpoena for Alamea's cell phone records, and went through a dozen more calls and emails from people who thought they had information on the dead girl. None of them panned out, though.

One man insisted that Alamea had been killed by the Night Marchers. "I saw them take her," he wrote, in an email. "They're going to come for me next."

Another woman who left a voice mail said she was a psychic. "I didn't see any mention on the newscast of her baby. Make sure someone takes care of the baby."

Ray shook his head. "These people come up with the craziest things."

The subpoena for Alamea's phone records was signed and faxed over to the phone company, and the woman I spoke to promised to have them together by the next morning.

By the end of our shift we were no closer to finding out who killed Alamea. Ray looked at his watch. "I've gotta go. We're meeting the priest at the church to go over the details of the baptism."

Ray and Julie were practicing Roman Catholics, and Vinnie was to be baptized on Saturday, at a Catholic church near their home in Salt Lake, close to the Aloha Stadium.

Ray and I had been working together for three years, and we'd become close friends off the job as well. Mike and I often went to dinner with him and Julie on the weekends, and before Vinnie was born they had asked Mike if he would be one of the baby's godfathers.

"My youngest brother is flying in from Seattle to be one," Ray had said. "But we'd like to have someone local, too. Has to be a Catholic, as you know."

Mike had been flattered. His father was Italian and his mother Korean, and both of them were practicing Catholics. Mike had grown up in the church, though he didn't go to mass except for the occasional holiday. By coincidence, the church closest to Ray and Julie's house, St. Filomena's, was the one Mike's parents attended, because they offered mass in Korean. So it all worked out very nicely.

"Have fun," I told him. I drove home, where I fed and walked Roby. Then I joined Dakota and Mike next door for dinner with Mike's parents. I had developed a real taste for Korean barbecue since I met Mike, and no one made a better marinade for the beef than Soon-O. Her special mix of soy sauce, garlic, sugar, sliced onions and some other spices was better than any restaurant's.

Dominic and Soon-O were so proud that Mike had been asked to be Vinnie's godfather, and they were looking forward to the ceremony on Saturday morning. "Almost like having a grandchild," Soon-O said. "But not quite."

I glanced over at Dakota. Was he, too, "almost like a grandchild"? Dominic and Soon-O had stepped up to help when Dakota came to live with us. Dom was a handy guy, and he'd been showing Dakota how to fix everything from stopped-up drains to loose towel racks. It was great for Mike and me; Mike hated that kind of thing, and I was oblivious to problems until things broke in some dramatic fashion.

Dakota didn't seem fazed by Soon-O's remark, unless you counted asking for another helping of barbecue.

Mike and I had been approached by Cathy, the poet from the Teen Center, and her partner Sandra, to be their sperm donors, and he and I had been going back and forth on the question. I was happy being Uncle Kimo to my nieces and nephews, while Mike was leaning toward becoming a father. Mike was an only child, and his parents, now that they were comfortable with his being gay, were eager to get themselves a grandchild however they could.

I was determined to resist the pressure. "Poor Ray looked like walking death this morning," I mentioned, between bites of the succulent beef. "Vinnie's keeping them both up all night."

"Mike slept through the night as soon as we brought him home from the hospital," Soon-O said. "What a good baby!"

"He does have a knack for sleeping," I said. Mike's favorite hobby was dozing on the sofa, with the TV going in the background. I was the more active one, always ready for surfing, jogging, or a more horizontal form of recreation.

"Your parents are probably too busy with all their grandchildren," Soon-O said. "But Dom and I would always be available to help you out. We love having Dakota, and I'm sure he'd be happy to help, too."

"Back in Jersey, I used to babysit for my cousins," Dakota said. "I already know how to change a diaper."

Little traitor, I thought, but I smiled, nodded, and kept eating. That night, Mike and I walked Roby together at eleven, giving him a last chance to empty his bladder before sleep. The dark sky was clear and spangled with stars, and I wondered what kind of wish Mike was making on them. Was it that important to him to have a child of his own? Why didn't I feel the same way?

We walked back inside and Mike surveyed the living room. "You're a pig, you know that?" he asked. I'd left my aloha shirt on the sofa when I switched to a T-shirt, and the morning paper was still strewn around the kitchen table in sections.

"Oink, oink." I grabbed for his hand. "Leave it. Let's go to bed."

He disengaged from me. "I can't go to sleep when the house is a mess."

I almost said that we couldn't make a baby together if we didn't have sex—but then I remembered the plumbing problem. I left him in the living room to clean up. I stripped down and slid between the covers, and I was asleep before he came in to join me.

The next morning I called the Medical Examiner's office soon after I got to work. "Hey, Alice," I said to the ever-cheerful receptionist. "Doc have the report together on the jigsaw puzzle girl?"

"He didn't like that one," she said. "You should have seen him. Grumbling and complaining all day. I'll transfer you."

I sat through some gloomy elevator music until Doc picked up. "Cause of death was massive blood loss due to internal hemorrhaging," he dictated. "Time of death was sometime between ten o'clock and midnight Saturday night. I don't have the full toxicology results back yet but she consumed a massive amount of sedatives shortly before death."

"So the killer knocked her out first?"

"That's not the best part. Your victim gave birth shortly before her death."

"Excuse me?"

"You heard me. All the results are correct. Where's the baby?"

"Great question, Doc. I have no idea."

I did have an idea, though. I went back through the phone records from the day before. The psychic had left her number, and I called her back. I introduced myself and asked if Ray and I could come over and talk to her. She agreed, and gave me her address.

It was my turn to drive, so we hopped in the Jeep and opened up the flaps. It was a sunny, cool morning and it felt great to be outdoors. We trailed behind an elderly man with a long gray ponytail, riding a slow-moving scooter, and I didn't mind because I knew we'd get where we were going too quickly anyway.

The old guy pulled in at a low-rise office building, and I

continued at the same sedate pace until we reached a run-down house in the shadow of the H1 expressway, beside a sign that read "MADAME OKELANI. TAROT CARDS, PSYCHIC READINGS, '*AUMAKUA*." The 'aumakua were also known as spirit animals in the Hawaiian tradition; they were the spirits of our ancestors, who had chosen to take physical form in the body of a particular creature.

Ray made a disgruntled noise in the back of his throat, like the one my father used to make when my brothers and I were kids and we were trying to put one past him.

An elderly Hawaiian woman opened the door. Her gray hair flowed down to her shoulders, and she wore an oversized muumuu in a rainbow of bright colors.

"I'm so glad you came, detectives," she said. "Sometimes law enforcement is distrustful of psychic abilities."

Madame Okelani sat down at a square table, and motioned us to the chairs opposite her. "How did you know the young woman who was killed?" I asked.

"I didn't know her. I just had a vision." She looked at us. "Do either of you have any experience with psychics?"

"I had my tarot cards read in college," I said. "That's about it."

"I think everyone has some level of psychic talent." She smiled. "I teach workshops on how to get in touch with your own ability, and one of the exercises I give people is to consider a news report, often one about a crime."

"I don't understand," I said. "Why crimes?"

"Because there will usually be follow-up reports, and those can verify information you might sense. For example, last week I saw a report about a burglary down the street. I was upset by that, because it was so close. I meditated, and I saw something very unusual—a mop and a pair of rubber gloves. I didn't know what to make of that. Then the next day I learned that the maid had been involved in the robbery."

"Did you report that information to the police?" Ray asked.

She shook her head. "Detective. If I called you about that you would have laughed and said I was crazy."

"But you did call us about this vision."

"Here's what I did. I saw the piece on the TV news about the girl you needed to identify. As soon as I did, I turned the TV off and went into a meditative state. I closed my eyes, lowered my heart rate, and tried to focus on the girl's energy."

"And you did this why?" Ray asked.

"I make my living this way, Detective. It's important that I be able to do as much as I can for my clients. And that requires discipline and practice."

"What did you see when you focused?" I asked.

She shuddered. "A lot of blood. But also a very tiny baby, like a newborn, red-faced and crying."

"Where was this?"

She motioned to a laptop on the table between us. "I use Google Maps. I open the program and then continue my meditation, hoping to be directed to a particular place on the map." She looked up at me. "The violence was too strong for me to focus. All I could tell was that the place I was seeing was near the water, with fishing boats. Perhaps a marina."

We hadn't released the location of the body to the press or the public, so it was interesting that Madame Okelani was able to get so close. Was she really a psychic? Or was she the one who had killed Alamea?

I could tell Ray was thinking the same thing. "Where were you Saturday night?" he asked.

"Why?"

Neither of us said anything, just looked at her.

"I attended a psychic fair at the Blaisdell Center on Saturday." She turned and retrieved a flyer from a counter near her, and passed it to us. "The fair went until eight o'clock at night, as you can see. An event like that can be very draining for a psychic, with so many people and so much to interpret. Several of my colleagues and I went out for dinner afterward, to regroup."

"What time would that have been?" I asked.

"Let me check my purse." She got up and left the room, and returned a moment later with a leather wallet. She pulled a receipt out from a restaurant at the Ward Center, time stamped 11:30 PM. "I guess we were there later than I thought," she said, showing it to us. "I can give you the names and numbers of the people I was with. And the server will remember me, too. She's a client."

I opened my netbook and took down the information. Madame Okelani had an unsecured wi-fi connection, and while I had the computer open I checked my email and downloaded Alamea's cell phone record.

"How is the child?" Madame Okelani asked when I was finished.

I shook my head. "We don't know. We didn't even know there was a child until we got the autopsy report this morning. Which was why we were surprised that you knew yesterday." I hesitated for a moment, unsure of how to proceed.

Like Mike, Ray had been raised a Catholic, and he had an innate distrust of anything that didn't fit within his set of beliefs. But I was more open in what I was willing to consider.

My parents were a polyglot mix of religion and ethnicity. My mother was half-Hawaiian and half-Japanese, and had little training in either culture. My father's father was a full-bloodied Hawaiian who converted to Mormonism and later married a white missionary from Idaho. My father had grown up believing in what he learned from both parents. He and my mother married in the Kawaia'aho Church in downtown Honolulu, and we'd been taken to services there as kids for the big holidays like Christmas and Easter.

But like my father, I'd taken it all in and remained independent in my beliefs. I had a strong set of spiritual beliefs, about treating your fellow man the way you'd like to be treated, and I respected the ancient gods and goddess of Hawai'i—Pele, who ruled the volcanoes; Kanaloa, the god of the seas; and Lono, who brings rains, fertility and harvest, among them.

"Can you try to focus on the baby again?" I asked. "With the computer?"

"Kimo," Ray said. "Can I speak to you outside?"

"I'll boot up the computer," Madame Okelani said. I stood up and followed Ray outside to her front lawn.

"Why are we wasting time here?" he asked. "The woman's a crackpot who had a couple of lucky guesses."

"You have any other ideas?" I held up my hand. "We have a dead woman who had no friends, and a newborn out there somewhere. Madame Okelani may be able to help."

"What about the records from Alamea's cell phone? We can work on those."

"Humor me, all right? Let's see if she can come up with anything."

We went back inside. Madame Okelani's eyes were closed, and her fingers rested lightly on the laptop's keyboard. We watched her for a moment. Then she opened her eyes.

"I'm sorry," she said. "I can't get anything. There's some kind of interference." She looked at my netbook. "Is your computer on, detective?"

"Hibernating. Is that the interference?"

"May I?" she asked, holding out her hand.

I gave her the netbook, and immediately she put it down on the table, as if it had burned her fingers. "Makiki," she said. "The baby is in Makiki." Beads of sweat appeared on her forehead. "I'm sorry, I'm not feeling well. I need to lie down."

"Thank you for your help," I said, taking the computer back. Ray and I turned toward the door.

"Oh, and detective? You're not a pig, you're a dolphin."

It took me a minute to process that. "Yes, you're right. Thank you."

"What the hell was that about?" Ray asked, as we got into the Jeep.

"Which part? Makiki? Or the dolphin?"

"Whichever part makes sense."

I opened the netbook and turned it back on. "I had an argument with Mike last night. The living room was messy, and he called me a pig."

"And?"

I pointed to Madame Okelani's sign, as the netbook came back to life. "You know what an ʻaumakua, a spirit animal, is?"

Ray shook his head.

"The ancient Hawaiians believed that their ancestors remained around them, often taking shape in a particular animal. A family would be protected by that particular animal. A family that lived in up in the mountains might have an owl for an ʻaumakua. One that lived by the water, like my family did, might have a shark or a dolphin.

"My father always told us this story about how he was surfing when he was a teenager, and the wind came up very strong, suddenly, and he got knocked off his board. He was floundering in the water, couldn't keep his head up out of the waves. Then he felt something nudge him from below, pushing him toward land. It was a dolphin."

I opened the PDF file of phone numbers Alamea had called.

"He told us that the dolphin was our family's ʻaumakua, and it would always protect us when we were out in the water."

"And did it?"

"We're all here, aren't we? My brothers and I have all been caught by waves, tossed around and banged up. But we all survived."

"Uh-huh. What do the phone records say?"

I looked down. "On Saturday afternoon, Alamea called a cell

phone several times." I flipped to another page. "That number is registered to a woman named Charlotte Montes, with an address in Makiki. I think that's our next stop, don't you?"

"We could have figured that out without the crazy lady."

"Just because you don't believe doesn't mean she's crazy."

We drove down to Makiki, to a small stucco house on a tiny piece of land, with a chain link fence all around. The gate into the small front yard was locked.

I called the number from the printout, and through the open front window I heard a tinny rendition of Israel Kamakawiwo'ole's "N Dis Life." As the phone rang, a baby began to cry.

No one answered the phone, and the baby inside continued to cry. "I think we have reason to believe that Alamea's baby is inside this house and may be in danger," I said. "We need to take whatever measures necessary to check it out."

"I agree." Ray grasped the top rail of the fence, testing it. Then he climbed up and over, dropping lightly into the front yard. I followed him, less gracefully.

I unholstered my gun. "If we're right, the woman inside killed Alamea."

Ray nodded, and pulled his gun out as well. I stepped up and rapped on the front door. "HPD. Open the door, please."

There was no answer. All we heard was the baby continuing to cry.

I tried the handle. The door was locked. I nodded to Ray to go around the left side of the house, and I went right, toward the open window. I approached it carefully, peeking in from the side.

Through the screen I saw a baby in a crib in the middle of the room. And on the floor, a young dark-haired woman sat with her legs out in front of her. She was crying, too, though more quietly than the baby. "Charlotte Montes?" I asked.

She nodded.

"Can you open the door, please?"

"He won't stop crying," she said. "No matter what I do."

"We'll help you," I said gently, as Ray joined me. "If you can get up and open the door."

She took a deep breath and stood up. Without a backward look to the baby she walked out of the room, and a moment later she was opening the front door.

We both holstered our guns and followed her inside. The baby was still crying, and Ray walked over and picked him up from his crib. He began rocking the little boy and cooing to him, and soon had him calmed down.

In the meantime, I sat down at the kitchen table across from Charlotte. Up close I could see she was a bit older than I had thought, probably late twenties or early thirties. "How did you know Alamea Kekuahona?" I asked.

"From the drugstore. I used to talk to her sometimes. One day I saw her checking out pregnancy tests, and she told me she didn't believe she was pregnant."

Ray stood behind her, holding the baby in his arms and swaying gently.

"She didn't even want the baby. And I did."

I nodded.

"She wouldn't go to the doctor or anything. I told her that I was a midwife, and I would deliver the baby for her, and no one had to know."

"But you're not a midwife, are you?"

She shook her head. "I thought I would help her deliver, and then she would give the baby to me. But she started bleeding, and she wouldn't stop, and then she passed out."

She looked up at me. "I didn't know what to do. I wanted to call 911 but I knew if they came, they would take away the baby."

"So you let her die?"

"We were both so stupid. We thought the baby would come out and she could go home. When she passed out I got scared, and I took the baby and went for a walk. By the time I got back she was dead. I didn't know what to do—she was so big and I couldn't carry her anywhere. So I had to cut her up in pieces." She shivered and began to cry.

I sat there with my arm around Charlotte's shoulder as Ray called Social Services to take custody of the baby, and a squad car to take Charlotte downtown. Lidia Portuondo answered the call, and I knew she'd be kind, yet careful, with Charlotte.

As Lidia was driving away, the crime scene techs showed up and sprayed a mix of Luminol and a chemical activator in Charlotte's bathroom. The Luminol reacts with the iron in blood to show traces of any blood residue, even after the surface has been cleaned, and the activator causes the luminescence that reveals the traces. It works best on non-porous substances, like the nubby tile on the bathroom floor. They turned the lights out, and we saw a blue glow where Alamea's blood had spattered. They took some long-exposure photographs that documented the traces.

Fortunately Charlotte wasn't a great housekeeper; if she had scrubbed the entire bathroom with bleach or some copper-containing substance, the whole room would have reacted with the Luminol, giving us a false positive and effectively camouflaging any of the blood traces.

When the crime scene techs were finished we locked up the house and drove down to headquarters, where we read Charlotte her rights and she gave us a full statement.

≈≈≈

Alamea had never told Charlotte who the baby's father was. As next of kin, Betty signed the papers so the baby could be put up for adoption. Charlotte was arraigned on charges of negligent homicide and released on bail.

We moved on to other cases, but I couldn't help thinking about Charlotte Montes, and the lengths some people went to in order to have a baby. And Dakota, whose mother had tossed him away as carelessly as Charlotte had dumped Alamea's body.

Saturday morning, Mike and I drove to St. Filomena's with Dominic and Soon-O. It was our first opportunity to meet both Ray's and Julie's parents, who had flown in for the occasion, and it was funny to me how quickly Dominic and Mike blended into the crowd of exuberant Italian-Americans from Philadelphia. I was left on the sidelines with Soon-O.

"Was this what it was like when you guys lived on Long Island?" I asked her.

Dominic and Soon-O met in Korea, when he was a wounded soldier and she was his nurse. After some opposition from both sides of the family, they had married, and she had worked to put Dominic through medical school, living near his big family in New York.

"Yes," Soon-O said. "Except there was a lot more talk in Italian. Dom's parents were born there, you know."

I knew that Soon-O had been unhappy in New York, far from her family and her culture, and that Mike had been uncomfortable as a mixed-race kid. The Riccardis had moved to Hawai'i when Mike was seven, in an effort to make both of them happier. As far as I could tell, it had worked.

"I'm sorry Michael couldn't grow up around his cousins, on both sides," Soon-O said. "And now Vinnie will be the same, so far from family."

"We make our own family." I took Soon-O's hand. "Look at us."

"I know," she said. "I almost feel like your mother is my sister. And now, Michael will be connected to Vinnie, and to Ray and Julie and their families. That means we all will be."

I looked up and saw Ray at the door of the church, trying to get everyone to go inside. "Well, then, we'd better go in and join them," I said.

I gave one last thought to Alamea Kekuahona and her baby, and hoped that both of them would find loving families, in Heaven and on Earth, and then I joined my family of choice for the ceremony to welcome our newest member.

"These babies are squashing my kidneys, Kimo," Sandra grumbled, as she struggled up the walkway to the front door of my parents' house in St. Louis Heights, overlooking downtown Honolulu and the Pacific Ocean beyond. She was a stocky fireplug of a woman, with truck-driver shoulders and close-cropped hair, and as her belly swelled with the growing twins she looked more and more like a beach ball with a head.

Her diminutive partner, Cathy, followed behind her. She was half-Japanese, but that half was clearly dominant; she had a sheer fall of waist-length black hair and the fine hands of an artist—though her art was poetry.

Cathy was the more maternal one, but she had some problem that prevented her from carrying a child. After a long discussion, Mike and I had both given sperm, and Cathy had donated eggs. Several of them had been fertilized and implanted into Sandra's womb.

The first ultrasound showed us what Sandra was already feeling: she was carrying twins. The boy and girl, nicknamed Alpha and Omega for the time being—as the first and the last babies Sandra would ever carry—had taken over her life since then. She was a high-powered attorney with a Rolodex of every lesbian in the Aloha State as well as the political and legal clout to gain, and win, high-profile cases. But after six months her obstetrician had confined her to bed rest to ensure she could carry the twins to term. She had not reacted well to having her activities curtailed.

We had met together the week before to brainstorm names for the keikis. We liked the idea of sticking to the letters A and O, and settled easily on Addie for the girl and Owen for the boy. "What last name are they going to use?" I asked. "Selkirk-Guarino? Guarino-Selkirk?"

"We had an idea," Cathy said shyly. She pushed a strand of

black hair from her forehead. "We both hate hyphenated names. And we want the kids to know right away that they have four parents."

"We took the first two letters of each of our names," Sandra said. "Riccardi, Kanapa'aka, Selkirk, and Guarino combine to make Rikasegu. Cathy, Sandra, Mike, and Kimo make Casamiki."

"You have got to be kidding me," Mike said.

"Absolutely not. We're making our own rules about being parents, so why shouldn't that include names?"

"I kind of like it," I said. "Hawai'i is such a melting pot. Why not melt our names together, too?"

"You all are nuts," Mike said.

"Didn't you ever feel like your name didn't represent you?" Cathy asked him. "I know I did when I was a kid. My dad's name is Scottish, but I look like my mom."

The girls were determined, and Mike caved. "Fine. But let's go with Casamiki. Easier to spell and pronounce than the other one."

This early December luau, sandwiched between Thanksgiving and Christmas, was Sandra's last outing before popping the babies out. Roby romped around us, even as Dakota tried to corral him without success. As he scrambled after the dog, his board shorts slipped down showing the waistband of his boxers and his T-shirt rode up. If only I had known myself at his age as well as he did, how different my life might have been. It sometimes astonished me how much my world had changed in the five years since I'd been dragged out of the closet. And now, life was about to change again, for all four of us.

"Here you are!" My mother appeared at the front door, all five-foot-nothing of her in a bright blue muumuu, her coal-black hair pulled into a bun on her head. "I was worried you wouldn't be able to come."

My mother is a tiny dynamo, even into her seventies. She ruled my big, blustery father, my two brothers and me with an iron fist in a velvet glove, and though she doted on every one of her grandchildren she was eager to see Sandra add to that number.

My parents had organized this massive luau to welcome Sandra and Cathy into our extended family and provide an opportunity for everyone to shower the soon-to-be-born twins with baby gifts.

My mother took Sandra by the arm and led her inside, settling her in a comfy chair in the living room with an ottoman for her feet. Mike and I walked into the kitchen, where my aunts and my sisters-in-law jockeyed to get food out for the hungry masses. Dakota joined my nieces and nephews, who were swarming from the downstairs den through the kitchen and out to the back yard.

Mike and I detoured around the food prep and walked outside with Roby, then let him loose to speed over to a pack of family dogs hovering near the kalua pig roasting in a pit dug in the back yard. Family and friends were all around us, and quickly we were all chowing down as if we'd never eat again: Hawaiian specialties like my mom's chicken long rice, my sister-in-law Liliha's shark-fin soup, my godmother's sweet and sour spareribs and my aunt Pua's Portuguese sausage and beans. Mike's mother had brought *bulgogi*, a spicy Korean barbeque, and my mother and my sister-in-law Tatiana had been baking cakes and pies and cookies all week, which shared space with platters of fruit, tubs of mango sherbet and chocolate ice cream in coolers, and about ten different types of salted, dried and preserved fruits called crack seed. I don't know where the name came from originally, but it's almost as addictive as the cocaine derivative.

Keola Beamer was playing on the stereo, singing about his family rocking in a wooden boat, but I could barely hear the music under the laughter and chatter of too many family members in one place. Fortunately my parents' yard backs up on Wa'ahila Ridge State Park, and the kids made their own campground under the trees.

Sandra and Cathy were the center of attention. Everyone had either a gift or a piece of advice for the new moms. As the dads, Mike and I got our share—everything from jokes about our ability to change diapers to confidential suggestions to handle teething (a little brandy on the gums) and diarrhea.

After we finished eating, Mike and I sprawled on the ground next to the pair of lawn chairs where Sandra and Cathy sat. My mother brought a stepladder out of the house and set it up, then stepped up on it. Tatiana hurried over to steady her. "Quiet down, everybody!" she boomed, and we all turned our attention to my mom.

"Al and I have an announcement to make," she said.

My father got up from his chair and tottered over to her, leaning on his cane. I hoped I was as handsome as he is when I reached my eighties. His black hair had gone gray and there were lines on his forehead that weren't there ten years ago, but his half-Hawaiian, *hapa–haole* genetic mix had served him well.

With the boost from the stepladder, and my father's shrinking over the last few years, my mother was almost eye-to-eye with him. She took his hand. "You all know that we love this house, and we love being so close to our two oldest sons and their families. But it's time for a change."

"After nearly fifty years with this woman, she's finally letting me have my way," my father said. "We are going to sell this house and move into a condo by the water."

My father, both my brothers and I all had the native Hawaiian love for the ocean. Lui, Haoa and I had grown up surfing with our dad, and I think all of us were happiest when we were either on the water or at its edge.

"Where are you going, Tutu?" Haoa's eldest, Ashley, asked. She had inherited her mother's luxurious ash-blonde hair and father's height and love for surfing. At nineteen, she was trying to make a place for herself on the women's circuit.

"We're looking around Diamond Head," my mother said. "No plans yet. But it's time for us to start cleaning out this old house. And my boys know what that means. If you want something, you take it, or it goes for sale or to charity."

"There goes the Kimo shrine," Mike whispered to me, and I

elbowed him. It was true; my room remained as I had left it when I went to college in California—my surfing trophies and posters on the walls, my childhood books on the shelves.

I hated the thought of parting with those old memories—but Mike and I lived in a three-bedroom duplex which was already overflowing. We had converted our junk room into a bedroom for Dakota when we got the official approval as foster parents. The third bedroom was an office Mike and I shared, which would also serve as makeshift nursery when the twins were with us.

"That's all," my mother said, taking my father's hand as she stepped down from the ladder. "Now eat some more!"

Once the adults were groaning from eating too much, my mother organized her grandkids into a cleanup brigade. Dakota tried to slink away but she caught him. "Dakota! You are as much my keiki as everybody else. So you work too!"

He slumped his shoulders and pushed back his shoulder-length black hair, but I could see he was happy to be accepted as another grandson. Around us the kids carried the platters into the kitchen, emptied the trash and folded up the tables, and Mike and I tried to help Sandra stand up. "I'm as big as a house," she cried. "Your parents don't need a condo. They can just live in me."

We each stood to one side and lifted, with Cathy pushing from the rear. "Please, God, take these children out of me!" Sandra said.

Mike and I helped her totter out to the car while my mother loaded Cathy up with leftovers. "I want a Cesarean" Sandra said. "Now!"

"Buck up," Mike said. "Where's that butch little lesbian we all know and love?"

"She's gone. All that's left is a baby machine."

We shoveled her into the front seat of the car as Cathy came out of the house, surrounded by an army of keikis carrying plastic containers of leftovers and shopping bags full of unwrapped gifts.

"How are you going to manage all this at your house?" I asked. Cathy looked almost as tired as Sandra, with dark circles under her eyes. And the babies weren't even born yet.

"We have a nosy neighbor across the street. She'll come over and help us unload everything," Cathy said, as she shoved all the packages into the trunk. "We go to the doctor on Wednesday. If Sandy hasn't gone into labor by then he's going to induce."

"You want one of us to come with you?" I asked. Mike and I had gone to a couple of visits with Sandra and seen the ultrasound.

"Bring a forklift." She leaned up and kissed both of us. "Thanks. I'll confirm soon."

Mike and I stood in front of my parents' house and watched them drive away. "Every time I remember we're going to be dads, it scares the shit out of me," I said.

"If my dad and yours could manage, then so can you and I," Mike said. "Now come on, let's clean out some of your junk while we're here."

We trudged up the stairs to what had been my room. When I opened the door, though, I was surprised. "What happened to the Kimo shrine?"

All my stuff was still there—but instead of the immaculate neatness my mother had always maintained, the room was a mess. My single bed was piled with old clothes. The floor was stacked with boxes.

"This can't all be yours," Mike said.

"It sure can't. Mom!" I felt like a teenager again, stretching the word out to multiple syllables.

She came up the stairs behind us. "Oh," she said. "I didn't realize you would start taking away so soon. I've been using your room as a staging ground. You wouldn't believe all the stuff we've had stuck away in this house. Even things from my mother-in-law."

"Really?" I asked. My granny had always been a bit of an

enigma. She was a very proper white Mormon woman from Idaho who had come to Hawai'i as a schoolteacher, married my grandpa, a native Hawaiian, and given birth to six children, four of whom lived to adulthood. Granny died when I was eleven, so I didn't know her well, and I found her imperious and scary. She had always lived in the same small bungalow in the McCully neighborhood inland from Waikiki.

My dad's oldest sister, my aunt Elizabeth, had married a serviceman and moved to Kansas. His younger brother, Uncle Philip, was a non-conformist who didn't believe in marriage or having kids. He and his long-time girlfriend lived near their second sister, Aunt Margaret, and her family in Hilo. After Granny died my father was the only one left to claim anything, and he moved a few boxes of her stuff to our house.

"You want any of this?" my mom asked. "I don't and I know it will be terrible to convince your father to throw any of it away."

I opened the closest box and found a photo album of my father and his siblings when they were little. "Look at Dad!" I said. "How cute was he?"

Three boys and two girls sat in a wooden cart hitched up to a white goat with a long beard. I could tell my dad easily; he was the biggest and the cutest, holding the goat's reins like he was in charge.

I looked up at my mom. "I'll take these and sort through them."

Mike sighed. "I'll start carrying them downstairs."

We recruited Dakota to drag six boxes of family memorabilia out to my Jeep and stow them in the back. We said our goodbyes reluctantly, rounded up Roby, and then headed downhill to the highway that would take us home.

Dakota was quiet in the back seat, with Roby's head in his lap. "You have a good time today, Dakota?" I asked over my shoulder.

"It was okay."

"Just okay? Don't let Tutu Lokelani hear you say that. When she makes a luau she expects rave reviews."

"She's not my grandmother."

I looked in the rear view mirror and saw him slumped against the seat.

"Does that mean Mike and I aren't your dads?"

"Not for real. Not like the babies."

Mike twisted around to look at Dakota as I got onto the H1 highway, a broad strip of concrete that cuts through the heart of O'ahu. Except for the occasional palm trees by the side of the road, it could be anywhere in the United States.

"Kimo and I went through a lot of shit so you could come and live with us," he said. "Hours of parenting classes. Piles of paperwork. If you think we're giving up on you because our family is growing, you're wrong as can be."

"What does 'ohana mean, Dakota?" I asked.

We had a running joke in our household, a line from the animated movie *Lilo and Stitch*, about an alien who lands in Hawai'i and pretends to be a dog in order to fit in.

Dakota slumped farther down in his seat, his head down.

"Say it, Dakota," Mike said.

"'Ohana means nobody gets left behind," he mumbled.

Mike reached back to grab Dakota's hand. "And it means you're always going to be part of our family, our 'ohana. Forever. You understand that?"

"Uh-huh."

Roby sat up and licked Dakota's face, then tried to climb around behind him. "Get out of my hair, you goofy dog," he said, and all of us laughed.

By the time we got home, Dakota had gotten over his pout, and he carried all the boxes inside without prompting, stacking them in the office.

Monday afternoon Mike had to go up to the North Shore to get some evidence for a case he was investigating, and he picked Dakota up from school and took him along. I got home around four and after I walked Roby we went out to the back yard together. I relaxed in a big Adirondack chair and he sprawled at my feet as I began looking through the albums of my dad's childhood.

The sun was sinking behind the Ko'olaus, but the temperature was in the mid-seventies and a gentle breeze ruffled the leaves of the kuhio tree at the back corner of the yard. Someone was barbecuing, and the tangy scent of meat and charcoal floated by.

It was freaky the way my father looked so much like I did when I was a kid. When you looked at me and my brothers together, you could tell we were family—but each of us had taken a different dip in the gene pool. Lui looked the most Asian of us, Haoa the most Hawaiian. I'd always looked the most haole—and I realized, seeing my dad as a kid, that he had, too. The brother who was a year younger was almost his twin; he was the one who had died of pneumonia as a boy. How weird must that have been for my dad, losing a brother? I couldn't imagine life without Lui and Haoa around.

Under the albums were some failed attempts at quilting that my grandmother must have abandoned. The quilt on the bed Mike and I shared was the first one she completed, back when she was a newlywed. My parents had another, better quality one.

I was sifting through the fabric scraps when an old-time sepia photograph spilled out. My grandmother, looking impossibly young, wore a white wedding gown with a lacy veil over her forehead. To her right stood an older couple I assumed were her parents.

I peered closer, looking for evidence of my genetic makeup. My great-grandfather was a stern-faced man with light-colored hair cut short. He had big ears and a broad nose, and didn't look like anyone I'd ever claimed kin to.

My great-grandmother was an older version of my granny. I remembered that Granny wore her salt-and-pepper hair in a tight bun, and I saw she'd copied her own mother on that. They had the same widely-spaced eyes, the same tight smile.

Why was the picture sliced in half, cutting out my grandfather and his parents? I flipped it over and saw the photographer's mark—from Idaho Falls, Idaho.

That was interesting. I'd always thought my grandmother never returned home after coming to Hawai'i to teach. But if she was married in Idaho Falls, she and my grandfather must have gone back there.

I skimmed through the rest of the boxes. The only thing of interest was an old leather-bound book with *My Diary* in script across the front. When I opened it I found Granny's name, Sarah Carhartt, written in neat penmanship on the front page.

The sun had sunk below the horizon by then, and it was too dark to read, so I carried the diary into the bedroom, followed eagerly by the dog, who must have thought we were going in to dinner, and sat up in bed to read the old-fashioned handwriting.

> *I am about to embark on the adventure of my life. I will turn eighteen on May 15, 1933. The next day, I will marry George Harmon and I will accompany him on his mission to the Hawaiian Islands.*

Huh? George Harmon? What about my grandfather, Keali'i Kanapa'aka?

Roby began barking, and I heard the front door open. "Loocie, we're home," Mike called, in his Ricky Ricardo imitation. I put the diary aside and went out to the kitchen, where Mike laid out a bucket of fried chicken. The three of us sat around the table and talked about Mike's investigation, Dakota's day at school, and the diary I had found.

Mike fed Roby a piece of chicken and said, "Your grandmother was married before? What happened to him?"

"I haven't gotten that far," I said.

Between cleaning up after dinner and helping Dakota with his homework, I didn't get back to the diary that night. I was curious enough, though, that I took it with me to work, on the off chance I'd get some time to read at lunch.

No such luck. Ray and I were roped into helping with the intake for a group of youth gang members, and I was swamped with that until just after two, when Cathy texted: *Sandy labor. QMC now.*

QMC was The Queen's Medical Center. I ditched the last of the paperwork on Ray and took off. My office at Honolulu police headquarters was close by, so I was there before Mike. I found Cathy at the nurse's desk in the delivery ward. "The doctor says she's only a few centimeters dilated, so it's going to be a while," she said. "But you know Sandy. She wants the babies out now."

"She's due for a major attitude adjustment," I said. "We all are. Babies live on their own timetable, not ours."

"Believe me, I know."

Cathy went back into the room to help Sandra with her breathing exercises, and I called my mom, and then Mike's, to give them the latest news. Then I paced around the waiting room until I remembered my grandmother's diary, on the front seat of my Jeep. I retrieved it and sat on a hard plastic chair to continue reading.

I started again with that first sentence. I had never heard that Granny had been married before my grandfather and I was eager to see if she got out of the upcoming ceremony. But she didn't; she described her wedding in mind-numbing detail, from the simple white satin gown with a "very stylish" matching cap, to everyone who attended the reception.

Granny was born in Utah and moved to Idaho Falls with her parents when she was ten. The stake, or Mormon congregation, had been there since 1895. The way she described the town reminded me of black-and-white Westerns I had seen—the old-fashioned buildings in the downtown, the prevalence of horses and cows. She loved to go out to the falls and sit there by the water contemplating the raw power.

Well, that was something she and I had in common, I thought. The love of water ran deep in our family.

I had never known that she had been brought up a Mormon; neither of my parents were religious, and they had raised my brothers and me with a general appreciation of all beliefs—we attended Christmas Eve mass at the Kawaia'aho Church downtown; honored the Kami—the nature spirits—of the four directions at the Shinto New Year's Festival; and studied the ancient gods of the islands at Hawaiian school one afternoon a week.

Reading between the lines, I discovered that Granny's family was wealthy, while George's was not. After hearing a returned missionary speak in Idaho Falls, George felt the call, but his family could not afford the cost of sending him to Hawai'i. It looked like theirs was a marriage of convenience; her father footed the cost of the mission, and Granny had the chance to escape Idaho Falls and see the world.

I skimmed past the details of her first night as a married woman until she was ready to leave home. There are some things we don't need to know about our grandparents.

> *My adventure begins! My first time on a train. As we leave Idaho Falls my parents stand at the station beside George's. Will we ever see them again?*

I put the book aside. That must have been so tough—to be an eighteen-year-old girl leaving everything behind for a new life somewhere else. How long did it take letters to travel from Idaho to Honolulu back then? The first trans-Pacific telephone cable was laid from Japan to the US via Hawai'i in 1934, but it must have been extraordinarily expensive to make calls.

I remembered my grandmother as a woman of few words,

but you wouldn't know it from her diary. She described the train compartment and everything she saw out the windows from Idaho Falls to Ogden, Utah. Then they transferred to the Union Pacific for the trip to San Francisco.

I scanned along, looking for information on the mysterious George Harmon—but there was very little. Occasionally she'd mention him in passing.

> *Every meal on the Streamliner is an event!*
> *George and I had the Nebraska Corn-Fed*
> *Charcoal Broiled Steak for dinner tonight,*
> *with baked potatoes and fresh corn, and a*
> *delicious lemon cake for dessert.*

So I knew what George was eating—but who was he? How did he feel about the marriage? None of that was there.

The swinging door to the visiting area bounced open and Mike strode in. "Where is she? Did she have the babies already?"

"Are you kidding? Cathy said she's only a few centimeters dilated, so it could be hours."

Mike shuddered as he sat down next to me. "I don't want to hear the clinical details. Just thinking of Sandra's vagina gives me the creeps."

"I can pull up some pictures online to show you," I said. "I know you've never seen one in person yourself."

"And you've seen way too many," Mike said. We had both been conflicted about our sexuality when we were younger. I slept with as many girls as I could, hoping to find the one who could erase my uncomfortable desires. Mike had never experimented that way, confining his sexual experimentation to a series of random encounters with men.

We heard a deep, throaty scream come from behind the closed door to the delivery room. "Let me say I am so glad women have babies and not men," I said.

"I hear you."

Mike had some phone calls to make, so he stepped outside. I promised to get him if anything happened, and went back to my grandmother's diary.

A true small-town girl, she was awed by San Francisco. She and George attended a worship service with a congregation in Oakland, founded by Mormons who had traveled to California around Cape Horn. While George met with the church elders, she spoke with a woman who'd visited the islands and learned about the louche customs of the people there.

> *The native women wear skirts made of grass!*
> *The Hawaiians are a simple people, content*
> *to live from the plenty of their land. But the*
> *church at Laie has made many converts.*

She described in great detail the cruise terminal where she and George boarded the Lurline for their trip to Honolulu. Then her diary stopped for several days.

I looked at the clock and realized that Dakota would be getting out of school soon. Most days, he took a bus from Punahou that dropped him at the base of Aiea Heights Drive, and he walked the last blocks uphill. He was responsible for taking Roby out, and then working on his homework until either Mike or I returned to fix dinner.

It didn't look like we'd be home by then. I called my best friend, Harry Ho, who lived down the hill from us with his wife and son. "Yo, brah," I said, when he answered. "Can Dakota have dinner with you guys tonight?"

"Sure. What's up? You both working?"

"Nah, Sandra's the only one doing the work today."

"For real? She's in labor?"

"Yeah."

"Good luck. Arleen says she was in labor with Brandon for

nineteen hours."

I groaned. "So maybe Dakota and Roby could stay over with you tonight?"

"No problem."

"*Mahalo*, brah. I'll call him."

Life had been so much less complicated when I was single and living in Waikiki. If I worked late, all I had to worry about was where I would grab some fast food for dinner. But now with a partner, a foster son and a dog, there were always complicated arrangements to figure out.

Dakota was already on the bus home when I got hold of him and explained the situation. "Sure. I'll go up home and get Roby and then go down to Harry and Arleen's. I owe Brandon a rematch on Fluorescent Fighters anyway."

He was only four years older than Brandon, and the two of them got along pretty well. "Cool. I'll call you later."

I hung up and went back to Granny's diary.

*I have been severely ill since we left the harbor. George attained his sea legs immediately, and he has been very kind, bringing me broth and plain toast whenever I have the stomach for it. I cannot help but consider, lying feverish in my bed, whether this is God's punishment. I must confess I do not possess the determination George has for spreading the Book of Mormon to the Hawaiian people. I just wanted to get out of Idaho Falls. But I promise, if I recover, to be the best wife I can be and devote myself to the Lord.*

Poor Granny, I thought. To love water the way she did—but find that being at sea made her sick. That had to be awful. And her doubts were touching. But I couldn't imagine a God who would punish someone who was trying to do good. At least let the poor woman get to Hawai'i!

Mike came back inside and we sat together for a while, both of us fidgeting. "What's going on in there?" he asked. Then his stomach grumbled. When I looked at the clock I realized it was almost six.

"You want me to ask the nurse?"

"Yeah."

I got up and walked down the hall to the nurses' station. "I wanted to check on Sandra Guarino," I said. "How's she doing?"

"Are you the dad?"

I nodded. "One of them."

To the nurse's credit she didn't even raise an eyebrow. "She's in the transition phase from active labor to delivery right now. She should be achieving maximum dilation within the next hour or so. She's carrying twins, right?"

I nodded. "Alpha and Omega."

"Interesting names."

"Oh, not their permanent ones. That's what Sandra has been calling them."

"Well, you should be able to speak to them directly within the next two hours or so. Maybe sooner. The doctor is monitoring her to make sure there aren't any complications."

Cathy had briefed Mike and me about the possible problems with twin births, like twisted cords or breech births. Most twin pregnancies lasted only an average of thirty-five weeks. If the twins popped out too early, their lungs, brain and other organs might not be completely ready for the outside world, and they would be more vulnerable to all kinds of infections and developmental problems.

We were lucky that Sandra had been able to keep them inside as long as she had; the babies should be a week or two short of full-term when they popped.

My stomach grumbled and the nurse smiled. "There's a vending machine down the hall if you want."

I thanked her and checked out the machine. I thought the turkey sandwiches would be safe; I got one each for Mike and me, along with chips and soda. "Thank you, Lord," Mike said, when he saw what I was carrying. "I didn't get to eat lunch and I'm starving."

"Here you go," I said, handing him his food. "But you don't have to call me Lord. Kimo will do."

"How about numb nuts?" he said, around a mouthful of turkey sandwich.

We gobbled our sandwiches and then Mike yawned. "I'm going to catch some Zs. Wake me if anything happens."

I looked at him. "You can sleep?"

He shrugged and closed his eyes.

I got up and paced around for a while, imagining all the complications. I just wanted Alpha and Omega to be healthy. I sent up a couple of prayers, to the various gods of my childhood, promising to be the best dad I possibly could.

Then I sat down with Granny's journal again.

> *My seasickness has passed at last. George tells me he prayed for me, so maybe his prayers, and mine, were answered. I was finally able to go outside today, and the ocean was so beautiful—a bright blue, sparkling in the sunshine, stretching on for miles and miles.*

Good for Granny. I was glad she could enjoy a bit of the trip.

> *This morning we docked at Honolulu. What a sight! The tall, stately Aloha Tower, and the Royal Hawaiian Band welcoming us*

> *with native music, streamers, and the flower*
> *necklaces called leis. Mine is just beautiful, a*
> *string of white and purple orchids that smell*
> *heavenly. It is awfully hot here, though! One*
> *of the elders from the stake in Laie met us*
> *and drove us to our new home in a Ford just*
> *like my father's. The simple cottage a few*
> *blocks from downtown is charming, with large*
> *windows and a broad, overhanging roof.*

I skipped ahead. Granny was unhappy in Laie. George was engaged in his mission every day, proselytizing and teaching. Granny was bored by the other Mormon women and their focus on home and family, and found them as provincial as the women of Idaho Falls. Laie was worse though, because at least in Idaho she had family and friends. And Idaho was not so infernally hot. Their house was not even close to the ocean. She complained about the strange place names and found the few native Hawaiians she met frightening.

Suddenly the door to the delivery room burst open, and two nurses and a doctor pushed Sandra out on a gurney. As they sped down the hallway, Cathy stepped out carrying a tiny baby wrapped in a blanket. She was wearing a hospital gown over her clothes and had a mask on a string around her neck.

"What's the matter with Sandra?" I asked her.

At the same moment, Mike asked, "Did she have the babies? Where's the second one?"

Cathy's face was streaked with tears. "The doctor called it abruption," she said. "The first baby came out, and then Sandy started losing a lot of blood."

Another nurse followed Cathy out of the room. "It's a separation of the placenta from the uterus," she said. "It's a common complication with twins, but it is serious. Are you the donor?"

She looked at me and I was about to say that Mike and I were both the fathers, but Cathy stepped in first. "I told her you and Sandy have the same blood type."

"That's true," I said. "We're both AB and Rh negative."

"That's the rarest type," the nurse said. She was a Filipina in her fifties, with a kind face and dark hair in a bun. "I'm not sure we'll have enough on hand for what she needs. Can you donate?"

"Absolutely."

"Good. Come with me."

I left Mike with Cathy and the first baby. I didn't even know if it was the boy or the girl. The nurse motioned me into an examining room and said, "I'll be right back."

I couldn't sit down. I was so worried about Sandra and the other baby. Would it be all right? I had no idea what the medical condition entailed, but from the way they rushed Sandra out of the delivery room it couldn't be good.

The nurse returned with an armful of stuff. "Have a seat," she said. "Read this form and fill it out while I get ready for you."

I took the paper and sat on the examining table. I skipped through the first part easily; I was healthy, and hadn't been in contact with anyone who wasn't. The second section was more complicated; I had to recall the details of the times I had been hospitalized, and remember the name of the pill I was taking for high cholesterol. I thought I was out of the woods when I finished that—until I came to the blood donation statement.

I had forgotten the bias blood banks had against gay men. When I came out of the closet I stopped giving blood as my own private protest against what I felt were archaic standards. I also stopped lying about my sexuality. I didn't walk around with a sign that read "I'm here, I'm queer, get used to it," but I answered questions honestly.

But if I answered yes to number seven on the form, that I'd had male to male sex within the past seven years—hell, within the past seven days—the nurse was going to tell me I wasn't qualified to give Sandra the blood she needed.

Fuck that. I checked "no" and completed the rest of the form and handed it to the nurse. She scanned it quickly, and I waited for her to catch me in my lie. After all, she knew that Mike and I were both the fathers of Sandra's babies, and she'd have to be clueless not to figure out what was going on.

But all she said was, "Give me your right arm."

I must have been fidgeting, because she said, "Please, sit still. Try to calm down. Sandra's going to be fine, and so are both the babies."

She didn't know that. But I closed my eyes and visualized my happy place, that deserted beach where I go with my surfboard, ready to catch the best wave I can. I felt the needle but I didn't flinch. I kept my eyes shut and focused on the waves rolling in.

"All done," she said. "You can go back to your partner and your baby."

So she knew. I got up and thanked her and walked back down the hall to the delivery room. No one was in the hallway.

I peeked in the door. Mike and Cathy were sitting in armchairs next to each other. Cathy was holding the baby and Mike, wearing a gown like Cathy's only much larger, was already playing peek-a-boo.

I stepped inside. "Get a gown," Mike said, pointing to a pile on a table.

"Any news on Sandra?" I asked, as I pulled on the gown.

"Not yet," Mike said. "This is Owen. Our son." He held the newborn out to me, wrapped in a blanket. His little eyes opened and he stared at me.

"Oh my God," I said, and my heart did a flip-flop. "He's amazing!"

The door opened behind me and I had to jump aside as the Filipina nurse stepped in. "Sandra's out of surgery and she's in recovery now. If you all want to come with me you can meet your new daughter."

Mike handed Owen back to Cathy, and we followed the nurse

down the hall to another room. She pulled aside a curtain to reveal Sandra lying on a gurney. She looked like crap—her flyaway light brown hair was plastered to her scalp, and her eyes were red with tears. But she held the second twin clasped in her hands.

Mike stepped close to Sandra, and she handed Addie to him. I looked at the perfect little girl, and then at him, and when our eyes met, I began to cry. Mike followed me a moment later. Then Cathy and Sandra joined in.

"Look at us," Sandra said, wiping away her tears. "A bunch of crying fools."

"Very happy crying fools," I said.

Mike handed Addie back to Sandra. Cathy slumped into a chair next to the gurney, still holding Owen. I've seen victims of violent crimes who looked in better shape.

I popped out my cell phone and started taking pictures of the babies, which I emailed to all the grandparents along with the relevant details of time and weight. Each of us called our parents then, and the room was so noisy the babies began to cry. "Get used to this," I said to them. "You've come into a big, boisterous family."

A pair of nurses, drawn by all the noise, came in. "Time for both moms to get some rest," the first one said. "We'll take the little ones to the nursery. Are you breast feeding?"

"I'm going to try," Sandra said. "But I'm not sure this cow will have enough milk."

"We'll work things out," the nurse said. "Now you get some rest. Your babies will be hungry soon, and you need to recover from the C-section."

After a round of kisses between adults and babies, Mike and I walked out. It was close to eight o'clock. "Should we pick up Dakota and Roby?" I asked.

"You want to?"

"Actually, I was thinking we might have one last night without parental responsibility," I said. "What do you think about that?"

He grinned at me. "Does that involve the two of us getting naked?"

"You bet."

"Then I'm all for it. Meet you at home."

He leaned in and kissed me. "We're dads," he said. "I can't believe it."

"We've been dads since Roby came to live with us," I said. "We're just expanding the 'ohana."

I got home first; I always drive faster than Mike. Though he was only a couple of minutes behind me, I was already lying in bed naked, waiting for him. "That's something I'll never get tired of coming home to," he said, stripping his own clothes in record time and hopping into bed with me.

I turned toward him and we kissed. We both had five o'clock shadow and vending machine breath but it didn't matter. Both of us were hard and I felt the need pulsing through me.

After we were both satisfied, he rolled up next to me, with his arm around my shoulders and my head on his hairy chest. "Love you, babe," he said, then yawned. "Nobody's going to change that. Not even a pair of brand-new keikis."

"I love you too, sweetheart," I said.

He was snoring a moment later. I extricated myself from his arms and went into the bathroom, where I washed up. I couldn't sleep. I was too excited at the thought that our babies were in the world. So I sat at the kitchen table with my grandmother's diary.

I was eager to see how far the entries took her—would I see my grandfather there? The births of my father and his siblings? I skimmed through a couple of weeks of boring entries, Granny growing more and more disenchanted and unhappy.

> *Today George came home early because he was running a fever. I put him to bed with a cold compress and tried to provide the same care for him he gave to me when I was sick*

*on the boat.*

There were no entries for a couple of days.

*George continues to fade away and I feel powerless to do anything to help him. A doctor came up from Honolulu and said that he had never seen such a bad fever. The more time I spend by his bedside, mopping his brow, holding his hand, the more I realize how much I care for him.*

*He is such a good man, and does not deserve such an illness. He loves this island and its people, and I have come to see things through his eyes. When one of the Mormon ladies comes to sit with him for a few minutes, I walk to the ocean's shore and pray to our God, and the gods of the Hawaiians, to heal him. Those few moments by the water's edge are my own salvation.*

Another gap of a few days.

*I have not been able to write for some time because my heart has been too heavy. Just as I saw how much I cared for my beloved George, he was taken from me.*

*He was buried two days ago in the cemetery on the hill. Since then I have been in bed myself, prostrate with grief. Today for the first time I am able to sit up, take some broth, and pen a few words.*

*I do not want to go back to Idaho. There is*

*nothing for me there. Here, though, I may
be able to make a difference, and keep
George's memory alive. And I have come to
love this island as George did, from the rough
surf to the tempestuous winds to the endless
sunshine. The elders have suggested that I
go to Honolulu, where a Mormon family has a
spare bedroom, and I can find some work as
a teacher to support myself.*

I sat back. So that explained the story I had been told growing up, that Granny had come to Hawai'i as a teacher. Not exactly the truth—but then, I had learned from years as a homicide detective that the truth is rarely simple.

There was a single page left in the diary.

*Leaving Laie was harder than I expected. We
had so few possessions and yet everything
reminded me of George. A very nice young
native man named Keali'i drove up from
Honolulu to pick me up, and he helped me
sort through everything and load up his truck.
He was so very kind, and made this difficult
process so much easier.*

That was it—at least for this volume. I would have to search through the rest of the boxes to see if Granny had started another diary of her life in Honolulu. I was pretty sure that the nice young native man named Keali'i was my grandfather. I wanted to read more, to see how their love affair developed and how their family had grown.

I yawned, and looked at the clock. It was after one in the morning, and I'd had a very long day. Time to go to sleep and rest up for the new day—and for dealing with the new life ahead of me.

Hidden in the depths of the mini-park at the corner of Rycroft and Alder in downtown Honolulu, the body of a teenage girl had been hung from a stately kiawe tree, with what looked like a leather belt around her neck.

"Jesus," I whispered to Ray as we walked up. The call, relayed by dispatch to us from patrol officer Lidia Portuondo, had mentioned a suspected suicide, but Lidia hadn't described the victim. We'd already passed a couple of uniforms stringing up crime scene tape around the perimeter of the mini-park, so we thought we knew what to expect. But even to a couple of seasoned homicide detectives, a young person's death somehow mattered more.

The girl was slim but curvaceous, and she wore a tight-fitting minidress in a floral print. Her coal-black hair hung around her face like a curtain, her head twisted at an unnatural angle. Beneath her feet was a tumbled pile of rocks, and it looked like she had assembled them in order to get high enough to wrap the sheet around the branch, then kicked them away to let herself fall.

A plumeria lei had broken apart and its purple and white blossoms were scattered around the base of the tree, with a high-heeled sandal nestled into them.

Many Hawaiians call the plumeria the "dead man's flower" because people often buy them to drape over gravestones. I knew that some of the *hula halaus*, when they needed to make leis for a performance, went to the cemetery and took the plumerias.

It was just after seven a.m. on a Monday in January. Lidia Portuondo, crisp in her uniform, with her raven hair pulled into a French twist, stood beside the body, speaking into the radio on her shoulder. She ended the transmission and looked at us. A young woman with the round face of a Malay stood beside her, with a baby in a fancy stroller by her side. "This is Citra Chang," Lidia said, and introduced me and Ray. "She found the young woman this morning."

"I like to bring the baby here by the trees," she said, in a lilting accent. "But this morning, ooh!" She rubbed her upper arms as if she was cold, though it was already over seventy degrees out.

While Ray questioned the Malay woman and Lidia walked off toward her cruiser, I prowled around the tree, looking for clues. The girl looked like she was dressed for a party, and my first thought was that she was a prostitute. But her makeup was simple, her skin spotted with a few bits of acne, and she didn't have the hard look I'd come to associate with women who worked the streets. Her face was too angular, her nose too sharp, to call her pretty, but she wasn't hideously deformed, either.

A few feet away from the tree, I noticed a small pink purse. I pulled a pair of rubber gloves from my pocket and skinned them on, then knelt down.

The purse contained a cheap cell phone, a Hello Kitty keychain, a couple of tissues, and a student ID card from McKinley High School. I compared the photo, which showed a young woman full of life, smiling flirtatiously at the camera, to the body above me. It was the same girl. There was no evidence of birth control in the purse, no pills or suspicious powder.

Her name was Aulaney Kahika. Her first name meant 'royal messenger,' a piece of useless trivia I had learned as kid in Hawaiian school. I opened my tablet computer and used the air card to access the Internet, then logged into the police department database. I got one hit; Aulaney had been arrested for shoplifting, the case dismissed with a warning.

The record included her home address. I opened a new case file, pulled up a blank form, and entered Aulaney's name and address. I used the camera inside the tablet to take digital pictures of the area and the body.

This case looked like another sad teen suicide to me; there had been a lot of those in the news in the recent past. But I wanted to do a full investigation. I had always had a soft spot for crimes against children, which had been deepened since taking in

Dakota as a foster son, and then the birth of Addie and Owen.

Lidia came up to me as I was struggling to get close-ups of the branch and the knot. I didn't want to disturb the crime scene by rearranging the stones to step on them. "I had this plastic stool in my trunk. Thought you could use it."

I thanked her and stepped up, wobbling until I had my balance, and took my pictures. Ray joined me at the tree as I was stepping down. "I called for a crime scene team and notified the ME," he said. "What have you got?"

"Not much yet." I lifted each of her arms and examined them for track marks. I didn't see any. "Rigor's already set in," I said. "So she had to do this at least three hours ago."

I stepped down and examined the backs of her knees—no track marks there either.

"If it was a suicide, then it makes sense that the girl might have crept out of her house while her family was asleep," Ray said.

"I got an address for her, only a few blocks away, so she could have walked easily. She was pretty well-hidden back here. What did that woman say? Is there usually a lot of traffic in this park in the morning?"

He shook his head. "She said she brings the baby here because it's so quiet. Doesn't usually see anyone at all, despite the fact that we're in the middle of the city."

It was gruesome to leave Aulaney hanging there, but it was best for the ME to handle taking her down in order to preserve evidence. I did notice several bruises on her arms and legs, and wondered if someone had tried to hurt her before she hung herself—or if someone had been there to help with the hanging.

Ryan Kainoa, one of the crime scene techs from headquarters, arrived in his van. I walked over as he was shoving his long black ponytail under a baseball cap. "Can you see if you can lift any prints from the girl's body?" I asked. "She's got some bruising on her legs."

We walked over to where the body still hung. "She's got smooth skin without hair," he said, pointing to her legs. "The humidity will help. I'll see what I can do, and I'll tell the ME's techs to be on the lookout, too."

He pulled out his print kit and began to work. A few minutes later, the ME's van arrived and the techs began the painstaking process of cutting the belt and lowering the body to a portable stretcher. Ryan moved on to a systematic search of the area.

Ray and I found a wrought-iron bench in the shade of another spreading kiawe, and I pulled out Aulaney's cell phone.

Ray read the numbers off to me, and I two-finger typed them into the file on my tablet. "I'm willing to bet most of the numbers here came from beaters," Ray said.

A beater was a cheap, pay as you go phone popular with criminals. "You think so?" I asked. "She's just a kid."

"Kids still want to keep secrets from their parents," Ray said. "If your phone is on Mommy and Daddy's cell plan, they can see your texts and the numbers you call, how long you're on the phone and when."

I wanted to get to know Aulaney better, so I used the air card for my tablet and signed into my Facebook account, where I searched for Aulaney's name. She hadn't restricted her page to friends only, so I was able to see the posts she had made, and that had mentioned her. It was pretty depressing.

Aulaney's last post had been several months before, but other McKinley students were still adding comments. A number of girls called her slut, bitch and whore; warned her to stay away from specific boys, and told her that she was fat and ugly, though she was neither. Girls had posted photos of Aulaney with graffiti over them—mustaches, devil horns, and nasty epithets. A girl named Marie White had even composed a little poem: "Cards on the table, books on the shelf, do yourself a favor and kill yourself."

I copied all their names into my record, wondering if Aulaney had followed Marie's advice.

"Looks like she fits the profile of a suicide," Ray said.

"But did she kill herself because of all this bullying? And if that's the case, can we get the kids who did this to her?"

"We're going to have to try," Ray said.

The ME's techs took Aulaney's body away, and Ryan finished his investigation. Ray and I made our way out of the park, past the uniforms who were keeping the curious away. A tall, broad-shouldered Japanese kid said, "Yo, what's going on in there?"

He was accompanied by a slightly younger kid who looked so much like him that they had to be brothers. "Police business," I said.

"There really a dead girl in there?" he asked.

I pulled out my badge and showed it to him. "You know anything about her?"

He backed away. "No, man. Nothing. We're just on our way to school, saw the flashing lights and all."

"How'd you know there was a dead girl in the park?" Ray asked.

One of the uniforms, a big lummox named Saunders, said, "That was me, detective. I know, I shouldn't have said anything."

I looked at my watch. It was after nine o'clock by then, and McKinley High was still a few blocks away. "Shouldn't you be in class now?" I asked the big kid.

"First period free," he said. "But we're going. No sweat."

Ray and I drove the few blocks to Aulaney's address, a run-down apartment building with flaking paint. A heavyset Hawaiian woman sat in a wheelchair out front, with a breathing tube in her nose and an oxygen tank hanging from the chair. "Aloha, Auntie," I said, as Ray and I walked up. "You know where the Kahikas stay?"

"Number six, in the back," she said. "But nobody there." She wheezed a few times and I hoped we weren't giving her an attack. "Girl at school. *Makuahine* work at laundry in Chinatown."

That would be the girl's mother. Ray split off to walk around the property and I squatted beside the woman. "*Makua kāne?*" I asked, wondering if there was a father in the picture.

She shook her head.

"You know the name of the laundry?"

She wheezed again. "Yuck you."

For a moment I thought she was cursing at me. "The laundry is called Yuk Yu?"

She took a deep breath. "Yuk Wu."

"Thank you, Auntie. Can I get you anything?"

She pointed at the yellow plumeria tree at the edge of the yard. It was just beginning to blossom. "Pick me a flower?"

I was reminded of the plumeria blossoms around Aulaney's feet. It took some reaching and jumping, but I was able to grab one of the yellow and white flowers and hand it to her. She sniffed it and smiled, then stuck it behind her ear.

Ray returned from his surveillance walk. "Ground level windows are all barred," he said. "If the girl left home last night, had to be by the door."

Ray used his cell phone to get the address for the Yuk Wu Laundry while I drove. I parked at a hydrant on Hotel Street and put my police decal in the windshield, and fished around in the back for a set of the printed forms we used to ask next of kin to release medical records and personal effects.

We found the laundry tucked away in an alley. The doors were propped open, with a huge standing fan blowing the warm moist air around.

I showed my badge to the Chinese woman at the counter. "HPD. I'm looking for Mrs. Kahika."

She turned behind her and bellowed, "Pua!"

Pua Kahika was probably only in her late thirties, but stringy hair and exhaustion made her look older. I introduced myself and Ray and asked if we could speak outside.

"This about Laney?" she asked. "She in trouble at school again?"

I nodded toward the door, and she followed Ray and me outside. "There isn't an easy way to say this," I said. "I'm afraid Laney is dead."

"Cannot be!" she said. "I just see her last night before I left for work. She was home in her bed."

Tears welled in her eyes, and she reached up to dry them. Ray pulled a tissue from his back pocket and handed it to her, and the tears turned into full sobs. "What happen?"

In the most careful terms I described how we had found Laney that morning.

"I always tried to do my best for my baby girl," Pua wailed. "Why would she do something like this?"

While I stood there with my arm around Pua Kahika, Ray went inside and returned with a molded plastic chair and a bottle of water. We sat Pua down and I squatted beside her. "Was Laney depressed at all?" I asked.

"Laney was a happy girl," she said. "Lots of friends. Very popular with boys."

Pua started to sob again, and Ray walked back inside. I held her hand until he returned with another chair. "I figured this would be a while," he said. "I'll get started on the forms she has to sign."

I sat in the chair facing Pua. "Last night," I said. "You said she was asleep when you left for work?"

"My shift starts at midnight," she said. "When I get home Laney is still in school. I go to sleep, and by the time I wake up she's in bed. I always check on her before I leave, but sometimes she stays out late with friends."

It was a sad story, one we often saw repeated when kids got in trouble. Parents worked long hours, leaving kids to fend for themselves. A friend of mine called them "latch-keikis."

"You know these friends?" I asked.

She shook her head. "Laney was a very private girl. She never told me much."

"Any serious boyfriends? Contact with older men?"

Pua shook her head to both. I gave her the phone number for the morgue, and one for a family counselor who could help her navigate the burial of her daughter. Ray handed her the release forms for her daughter's medical records and personal effects, and she signed them. She also gave us permission to use Laney's key to enter her home and look for any evidence that might indicate either suicide or homicide. Then we walked her back to the laundry and left her in the arms of the Chinese woman at the register.

The ME's report would either confirm or rebut the suicide theory, and while we waited for it, we wanted to get a better sense of this poor latchkey girl, and what might have driven her to hang herself.

We went back to the house. The woman in the wheelchair was still there, and we waved hello as we passed her. Ray and I put a fresh set of gloves on, then used the key from the Hello Kitty chain to open the front door. We walked into a small living room that had been cut in half by a makeshift curtain. A galley kitchen along one wall, single bedroom and bathroom.

I pulled back the curtain. It looked like Laney had carved out that area as her bedroom. A single bed was pushed against the wall, with a beat-up wooden dresser and one of those portable metal racks for hanging clothes. The dresses on the rack were similar to the one Laney had died in, short and slinky.

A poster of the Hawaiian reggae band The Green loomed on one wall; beside it was another for a concert by the group Soja. The other wall sported a tough-guy poster of George Veikoso, also known as Fiji, as well as a couple of glamour shots of Hawaiian homeboy Bruno Mars, big hair and all. Typical teenage girl.

We prowled the room looking for anything that might help us discover what had brought her to that park the night before.

It felt uncomfortable looking through her drawers, but I'd been a teenager once, and I knew the kind of places kids hid things.

"You see her underwear?" Ray asked.

"Yeah—mostly generic bras and panties."

"And these," he said, holding up a lacy black bra. "Found it at the back of the drawer. La Perla."

"Sexy," I said.

"And expensive. This is two hundred bucks, easy."

"Didn't realize you were such a connoisseur."

"What can I say? Julie has expensive tastes, and I humor her. Special occasions, you know."

I raised an eyebrow but didn't comment.

"And this bustier?" He held up a slinky black number I had a hard time imagining on a teenager. "At least a grand. Too rich for my blood. Where does a poor girl in a run-down apartment get stuff like this?"

"A rich boyfriend?" I asked. "With a motive for murder?"

"Or itchy fingers," Ray said. "Didn't you say that Laney had a shoplifting arrest? And it's always possible that these are knockoffs from the Aloha Bowl flea market."

I took some notes on my tablet, writing *boyfriend?* "So we've got a sexually adventurous young woman, but no birth control pills or devices. No diary that might have expressed suicidal thoughts. No alcohol, no pills."

"She didn't have much privacy here," Ray said. "So it's possible she kept everything secret hidden somewhere else. Maybe a locker at her high school."

I took a series of pictures of the room and we drove to McKinley, one of the oldest schools in Honolulu. My father had gone there; we had a picture at home of his class, perched on the steps outside the three tall arches that led into the main building. It still looked much like it did in that old photo, from the cupola on the top to the statue of President McKinley on the lawn.

We had to be buzzed inside, and went directly to the principal's office. Shirley Yip was a trim Chinese woman in her mid-forties, wearing a pink business suit and no-nonsense black pumps.

We introduced ourselves and explained about Laney's death. She shook her head with sadness. "The poor girl," she said.

"Was she a frequent visitor to your office?" Ray asked.

"Sadly, yes. Once Laney reached puberty, she started acting out—being overtly sexual. In one case she took a boy's hand and put it on her breast, in the middle of math class. I'm sure there were a lot of other incidents that didn't get reported."

She sighed. "One of her most persistent problems was wearing inappropriate clothing—filmy blouses without a bra underneath, skirts that were too short. Teachers sent her to me, and I sent her home to change."

I thought back to the skimpy minidress Laney had been wearing, and the similar ones on the rack in her bedroom. "What did her parents have to say about that?"

"Single mother, no father in the picture. I had the sense she didn't supervise Laney very much." Though she didn't say more, I had a feeling she knew a good deal about Laney's home life.

"Was she referred to a social worker or school psychologist?" Ray asked.

"Budget cuts hit us hard, detective. A single school psychologist commutes between here and two other high schools, and she spends most of her time testing students who are developmentally delayed and coming up with educational plans for them. There's no time for her to speak with a girl like Laney. Laney was assigned a counselor, but the focus is on academics and making sure that students are placed in the right career houses based on their future plans."

"Her mother said that she often stayed out late with friends," I said. "But from her Facebook profile, it doesn't look like she had many friends at McKinley. Do you know of any students she might have confided in?"

Ms. Yip hesitated.

"Right now we're trying to get a sense of who Laney was, and what might have driven her to commit suicide," I said.

"This is a big school," she said. "The students I know personally fall into two groups: the high achievers, and the troubled young men and women. So though I knew Laney and the problems she faced, I didn't have much contact with her outside my office. You might speak with her counselor, Mr. Gainsway."

"How about her locker? Can you get someone to open it for us?" I showed her the release form Laney's mother had signed, and she called a janitor, an elderly Japanese man who led us down a series of hallways festooned with posters and then used a master key to open the rickety metal door.

There wasn't much inside—a few textbooks, a couple of energy bars, and some other assorted teenage detritus. "No birth control here either," Ray said. "You think maybe she was trying to get pregnant? She wouldn't be the first lonely teenage girl to think a baby would give her the love she was missing."

I thought of the young lesbian I knew from my youth group, and how she had deliberately set out to become pregnant. But she had already finished a two-year course in marine maintenance, had a job and a place to live. Laney Kahika was living behind a curtain in her mother's run-down apartment.

"It's possible," I said. "The ME will tell us if she was pregnant. Maybe the boyfriend with the expensive taste in lingerie didn't want to be a father."

The janitor led us to Mr. Gainsway's office, where the counselor was meeting with a student. As soon as he was finished, Ray knocked on his door and introduced us. I stayed by the door and let Ray, who had the sociology background, handle the interview.

Gainsway was an eager young haole in his late twenties with thinning blond hair. "What a shame," he said, when Ray had explained about Laney. "She wasn't a bad student, you know. If she had focused her energies better, she might even have gone to college."

"What program was she in here?" Ray asked.

"The Academy of Hospitality and Tourism," he said. "It's a catch-all for students who don't have college aspirations, and don't have specific technical skills like auto mechanics."

"How well did you know Laney?" Ray asked.

"Not well. I may have met with her two or three times. But I'm responsible for hundreds of students, and it's hard to spend much quality time with any one of them."

"You'd probably remember Laney from the way she dressed," Ray said, and Gainsway blushed. "You must have seen her around school. Did she have friends? A boyfriend, maybe?"

"I did see Laney around campus. She was very flirtatious, with the boys, with her teachers, with me. The other girls didn't like her. But I couldn't tell you a specific student she was friendly with."

"How about bullying?" Ray asked. "Do you think she was a victim of that?"

"Teenaged girls can be vicious, detective, as I'm sure you know. I never witnessed any specific incidents, but I wouldn't be surprised if some of the girls lashed out at her."

We thanked him for his time, and went back to headquarters, where we sat down with Laney's phone again, hoping there might be more clues there to her mental state.

We scrolled through the rest of the stuff on her phone—free games, apps for the weather, for hairstyles and tracking her period, for creating stickers and even virtual cupcakes. I clicked the green icon for something called WhatsApp, a chat program with buttons at the bottom for *Favorites*, *Status*, *Contacts*, *Chats*, and *Settings*.

*Favorites* displayed with a small circular icon, the contact's name, and the first few words of their most recent message. None of them used real names except her mother, and none of them had actual faces, just generic gray-and-white face icons or cartoon characters. All of them had the word "mobile" beside the name, which I assumed meant that's how they were connecting to the service.

Either Laney had deleted all but her last eight "conversations," or they were automatically removed after a period of time. Each one was about hooking up. Different guys, different places. Boys with cars picked her up; those without either came to her apartment after midnight, or met her in places like the tiny park where we'd found her body.

It was horrifying to see Laney's low self-esteem played out in those bits of text. Even the boys who wanted to have sex with her called her names like 'ho' and 'cunt.' And yet she appeared to have met them and shared the most intimate part of herself with them.

There were no messages from the night she was killed, and nothing to indicate that she was suicidal. Ray had faxed over the request for Laney's medical records to the free clinic her mother took her to, hoping that there would be a referral there to a psychiatrist.

By then, it was the end of our shift, and I knew we wouldn't get the ME's report until the next morning at the earliest. Once we knew if we were looking at suicide or homicide, we'd know how to proceed.

I'd just gotten into my Jeep when I got a text from my nephew Alec, my brother Haoa's son. "Uncle K, cn I buy U a coffee?"

I called him back. "What's up?"

"Just wanted to hang with my favorite uncle," he said. "You get off work now, don't you?"

That was curious, that Alec would be aware of my hours. "I do. Where are you now?"

"Punahou." Alec attended the elite private school my brothers and I all had. "You think you could pick me up?"

We arranged that I'd meet him at the bus shelter across from the school's entrance, and I hung up. Traffic was less than I expected, and I got to Punahou a few minutes early, so I pulled up beside the school to wait for him. The fence around the campus was hung with posters and banners supporting candidates for student government. It was a great ad for the school's ethnic diversity—some Hawaiian names like mine, while others such as Cindy Chow, Annette Gomes, Mike Befeler, and Theo Toyama showcased the wide range of student backgrounds.

Alec appeared and jumped into the seat beside me. He was about sixteen and very handsome, with his father's height, his mother's blond hair, and a slim build like mine. I put the Jeep in gear and headed toward a nearby branch of the Kope Bean, our island Starbucks.

We hadn't gone more than a half a block before he asked if I had any condoms.

"Whoa!" I said. "Where did that come from?"

"My friend Theo hooked up with this girl and he tried to buy condoms at a drugstore before he, you know, did it, with her. But the clerk said she wouldn't sell to him because he was too young." He looked down at the Jeep's floor and scuffed it with the toe of his sneaker. "Theo said it didn't matter anyway because the girl was on the pill, but I know there's other things to worry about."

"That's absolutely correct. Even if the girl says she's on the pill, she could be lying or she could have some kind of disease."

"I know. We learned about AIDS in health class."

"And the transmission of gonorrhea, and syphilis, and chlamydia, and…"

He interrupted me. "I know, I know. You're the cool uncle, and you're probably having sex all the time, so I figured you could give me some."

I pulled over into the parking lot of a karate dojo and turned to my nephew. I had no intention of discussing my sex life with him, but unless I pushed him back to his dad, somebody had to talk to him about his.

"I'm not going to lie to you. Sex is very cool and fun, if you have it for the right reasons. Because you really like someone, because you care about her, because you want to share this amazing experience."

He looked at me with a wide-eyed stare.

"But it's not so good if you do it with someone you don't like, or you do it so you can say you have. Believe me, I know. And the most important thing of all is to treat the other person with respect. You are sharing this experience, and the way you act toward each other can make it great, or terrible."

When I was sixteen, I probably would have said something like "Yeah, right." Back then, I got hard-ons all the time, from thinking about boys, seeing girls' breasts, rubbing against the sheets of my bed, anything. Sex was a huge mystery to me, for years, even after I started having it.

I sighed. There was nothing I could tell Alec that he didn't already know, that he hadn't heard or seen on TV, in school, or in whispered conversations with friends. "I don't have any condoms on me," I said. "But I can take you to a drugstore." I put the Jeep back in gear.

"That would be cool. Maybe you could tell me about the different brands and sizes and stuff. You could call it a trial run for going with Owen someday."

As I pulled back into traffic, I shuddered at the thought of my adorable baby boy grown up to be a teenager. Would he be gawky and pimply? Handsome and sociable? Gay or straight?

I headed to one of the big discount stores that I thought would have a good selection of condoms. "So, before we get there," I said. "Do you know if you're allergic to latex?"

"I'm not. We use latex gloves in science class sometimes."

"Good. Latex condoms are stronger than polyurethane, and so they give better protection. Because penis size fits a bell curve, most guys are in the middle, so they're mostly average size. But I suggest you try one out on yourself in private, to make sure. You don't want one that's too big to come loose, or one that's too small to break."

Alex fidgeted in his seat.

"Is this making you uncomfortable? Would you rather I had your dad talk to you about this?"

"No!" he said quickly, and I laughed.

"Okay. Remember, you need to use a condom any time your penis goes into someone else's body."

"Even the mouth?

"For now, yes. Once you get more experienced, and know what's what, you can make your own decisions."

I parked in the megastore's parking lot and we walked to the pharmacy section. I picked out a box called the Pleasure Pack that included a variety of different styles, and a bottle of the lube that Mike and I used. Alec began to pull out his wallet, but I said, "First box is on me."

I felt weird buying the stuff with Alec beside me, as if the cashier might think I was some kind of pedophile. Probably over-reacting, but once I came out of the closet in a very public way, a lot of people in Honolulu made judgments about me. "I'm going to get the pharmacist to ring me up. Why don't you wait for me by the front door?"

I paid, and when we got out to the Jeep Alec stuffed the bag in his backpack. I swung up into St. Louis Heights and dropped him where the Punahou bus would have left him off, and watched as he crossed the street and began to climb the hill. If I was worried about him, I couldn't imagine how I would feel when Addie and Owen were his age.

That evening Dakota was out on a group date with a bunch of friends, so Mike and I had dinner, just the two of us. I told him about taking Alec condom-shopping. "You didn't," Mike said.

"Did. And I promised I wouldn't tell his parents unless he screwed up somehow."

"Did you at least talk to him about safe sex?"

"I figured he already knew that, because he was asking for condoms." I told Mike what I'd said to Alec, about caring for the person you had sex with.

"Can't argue with that," Mike said, and he smiled at me in a way that said if I was a good boy I might get lucky later.

To quell my rising erection, I shifted focus and told him about the case Ray and I had caught that morning. "It was so sad to see the nasty things kids posted about her."

"That's what kids do," Mike said. "When my parents and I lived back on Long Island, kids used to make fun of me because of my eyes. Called me chink and chopstick and monkey boy. That was one of the big reasons why we moved to Hawai'i."

"I always thought it was because your mom was so unhappy there."

"That, too. But it was mostly that neither of us fit in with my dad's family, who were all a hundred percent Italian."

He drank some wine. "I got lucky here. Made friends right away and fit in, because I was athletic. But one guy in my class had a harelip. Some of the kids teased him, and junior year he took his father's shotgun and killed himself."

"That's terrible." I reached across the table for Mike's hand. "We have to make sure that Dakota and Addie and Owen always know that they are loved, that we have their backs," I said. "No matter how they turn out."

"I have no problem with that," Mike said, and the way he squeezed my hand told me much more than that.

The next morning, soon after I got into work, I got a call from Doc Takayama. "I've emailed you the results of Aulaney Kahika's autopsy," he said. "But I'll summarize the key points for you. Removal of the belt around her neck revealed a ligature mark below the mandible, approximately 1.5 inches wide. It encircles the neck in the form of a "V" on the anterior of the neck and an inverted "V" on the posterior of the neck, consistent with hanging."

"Okay," I said. I reached for my tablet computer and turned it on.

"Minor abrasions are present in the area," Doc continued. "Hemorrhage surrounding Ligature A indicates this injury to be ante-mortem and results in asphyxiation as the cause of death."

I drummed my fingers on my desk as I waited for the tablet to turn on.

"She had a high concentration of alcohol in her blood, which means that prior to death her coordination would have been quite impaired. In my professional opinion that would have made it difficult for her to perform the physical tasks involved in hanging herself. My judgment as to the method of death is homicide."

"Thanks, Doc. I'll check with Ryan and see what kind of evidence he found."

"One more thing, Kimo," Doc said. He hesitated, and I knew from experience that meant something bad was coming. "Though there was no evidence of recent sexual activity, we did some routine blood tests, and your victim was HIV positive."

"Wow. Sixteen and positive. That's grim."

"No grimmer than what I see on a daily basis," Doc said. "The sad part is that with the drugs available she could have lived with a low white cell count for years."

I thanked him, and hung up. "We've got ourselves a homicide," I said to Ray. The tablet was finally awake, and I connected to the department's email server. I opened the autopsy report Doc had emailed, and Ray joined me to read through it.

Once we were finished, Ray said, "We ought to start with the social media posts of teenagers who demonstrated that they had a grudge against Laney," he said. "I'll make a list of kids we should talk to."

While he did that, I went downstairs to see what Ryan Kainoa had been able to pick up from what I could now call the crime scene. I found him in the lab, his long black hair once more bundled up, now covered with a shower cap. "The hanging yesterday is a homicide," I said. "You have the evidence?"

"Sure." He turned to a worktable where a long brown leather

belt was spread out. "This is the belt. Size 46, but whatever manufacturer's name might have been on it has worn away."

"Man's or woman's?" I asked.

"Hard to tell. For the most part, belts are interchangeable. The buckle on a man's belt is always on the right side, with the holes on the left, like this one. But a woman's belt can have the buckle on either side."

"Any fingerprints?"

"Lots of prints of no value on the body and the belt," he said. "Too degraded or too partial. But I did get lucky and I was able to pull off a couple from the lower leg. Two right index fingers that don't match, which indicates two separate individuals."

I nodded. "I had that feeling. It's tough to string somebody up like that by yourself."

"I ran the prints through the state and federal systems for you, but I couldn't find any matches," Ryan continued. "I'm still processing fibers from the crime scene. I'll let you know if I come up with anything useful."

I thanked him and went back upstairs. Ray was on the phone when I sat down at my desk. As soon as he hung up, he said, "Got a fax from that free clinic. Laney hadn't been there for at least a year, and was never referred for either psychological counseling or any STD testing."

He sat back in his chair. "I pulled all the numbers from Laney's phone and started a subpoena for the records. But then I got caught up with this WhatsApp instant message program."

I sat beside him and we scrolled through Laney's history. The chat screen had a place for a photo of the contact, and the first few words of their conversation. The only contact with a photo or a real name was her mother. The others either had cartoon avatars, or no picture at all.

"Can you match any of these screen names to her Facebook contacts?" I asked.

"I tried. No matches."

"Do you think Laney knew that she was HIV positive?" I asked. "Could she have been spreading it around to boys at McKinley without knowing? Or was it a way of getting back at the kids who had teased her? All it would take would be for one of the boys she infected to pass the virus on to one of the girls, and it would spread from there."

"The only way to find out is to talk to the kids," Ray said. "We can start with the numbers in her phone. And if we have to wait for the phone records to come through, we'll be sitting on a cold case."

"Let's do it, then." We used Laney's phone to call each of the eight numbers she had exchanged text messages with.

None were answered, and only one had voice mail. "Leave a message if you have to, but remember to vote for Toyama for student government."

"That name sounds familiar." I struggled to remember where I'd heard it, and recalled sitting outside Punahou waiting for Alec, and all those multi-culti names on posters, including Theo Toyama. "I know who it might be."

I wondered if he was the same Theo who Alec had mentioned as a friend, and made a note to check with my nephew and warn him off the friendship, if necessary.

"So this private school student council wannabe was slumming with a public school girl," Ray said. "Spell the name for me."

I did, and while he searched the police database, I did some searching of my own.

"No record," Ray said.

I went back to my old faithful Facebook, and discovered from Theo Toyama's page that he had "friended" an uncle—who in turn had friended his brother, Theo's father. Once I had the father's name I was able to get a home address. "I'll swing by the parents' house on my way home," I said. "See what the boy has to say for himself."

Even though Theo Toyama had moved up to suspect number

one, we couldn't ignore other teens and other motives. "We haven't seen any evidence of a rich older boyfriend, so I'd say we stick to our two pools of potential suspects," I said. "Boys she hooked up with, and girls who hated her because she was easy."

Ray nodded. "If she passed on HIV to a boy, getting revenge on her is a powerful motive. And for a teenaged girl, stealing a boy's affection is almost as powerful."

"The belt that was used was forty-six inches," I said. "Too big for either Laney or her mom, and we didn't see any men's clothes at the apartment. You think that narrows the field at all?"

He shook his head. "Another girl could steal her dad's belt. Or just buy an old one at a thrift store."

"There's that," I said. "While you finish the subpoena for the phone records, I'll call the principal and get some interviews set up with the kids who posted on Laney's Facebook wall."

I called Shirley Yip and asked if she could assemble a group of students for us to talk with in conjunction with Laney's death. She agreed, and I faxed over a list of the names. When Ray returned from the judge's office after getting the subpoena signed and handed off to the phone company, we drove back to McKinley.

"I called and notified a parent or guardian for each of the students," she said. "I explained that you don't consider these kids suspects or even witnesses, so the parents don't need to be present."

"You've done this before, I guess," I said to her.

"All too often. I pulled the students from class and I have them waiting in a conference room," she said. "I'll have my secretary bring the kids in one at a time."

The kids all knew that Laney was dead by then, so we didn't have the element of surprise, and they were all wary. No one identified with any of the user names on her phone, and nobody was willing to admit to bullying her, even when confronted with the Facebook posts.

Marie White, the girl who'd composed the poem, said, "Somebody must have hacked into my profile. I'd never write anything like that about anybody."

"They're all angels," I said to Ray after Marie left. "None of them would even say a bad word to Laney, much less hang her."

"They're kids, and they're scared. Of course they're not going to admit to anything."

The last boy to come in looked familiar. Tall, broad-shouldered and Japanese, his name was Joseph Mishima. In my mind I went through all the juvenile offenders Ray and I had arrested in the past year but couldn't come up with a match. I figured the kid had a common look.

"Did you know Laney Kahika?" I asked.

He shrugged. "Just from around school."

"What did you think of her?"

He leaned in close. "She had this reputation, you know. That she was easy. A lot of the girls really hated her for that."

"You and Laney ever hook up?" I asked.

He wouldn't meet my eyes. "It's not a crime," I said. "Teenagers hook up all the time. And if you did, well, then you had to like her, right? At least a little. So you'd want to help us find out who killed her."

He shook his head. "Laney, she wasn't a good person," he said. "Whoever killed her did the world a favor." He pushed back his chair. "Can I go now? I've got an after-school job and I've got to get there."

"You can go," I said. I was afraid that if he stayed to answer any more questions I might show him what I thought of anyone who'd think a murderer did the world a favor.

It was the end of our shift by the time we finished at McKinley. "What do you want to do now?" Ray asked, as we walked back to the school's parking lot.

"I want to talk to that kid from Punahou," I said. "But I don't want to call attention to him by interviewing him at the school. I'll go over to his house."

There were no cars in the driveway, but the door was answered by a tall, skinny Japanese boy, with his dark hair pulled back into a ponytail that reminded me of Ryan Kainoa's.

I showed him my badge. "Are you Theo Toyama?" He looked fearful but he nodded. "I'd like to speak to you about an investigation. May I come in?"

Like the teens I had spoken with at McKinley, Theo was only a person of interest, not a suspect. And since we were in his home, and he was free to ask me to leave, I didn't have to read him his Miranda rights either. This was just a conversation.

"I recognize your last name," he said, as he led me into the living room. "Are you related to Alec Kanapa'aka?"

"He's my nephew." Since Alec was this kid's friend, I decided to approach this from the Good Samaritan angle, at least at first.

Theo sat down on the sofa. I sat on a chair across from him. "Theo, do you know a girl named Laney Kahika?"

He shrugged.

"I think you do, because I found your number in her cell phone."

"What does it matter?"

"Somebody killed Laney on Monday night, and I'm looking into everyone who knew her. You did know her, right?"

"Not well or anything. Just, you know, to say hello to."

"More than just say hello," I said. "If your number was in her cell. What did you think of her?"

"We didn't sit around and compare Zodiac signs or anything. She was all right, I guess."

The slow and steady approach wasn't working too well, so I decided to amp up the pressure. "So, how many times did you have sex with Laney?"

Theo paled but didn't speak.

"See, when the medical examiner did the autopsy he discovered that Laney was HIV positive. I know you had sex with her, and I wanted to tell you that if you didn't use a condom, you need to get tested."

His mouth dropped open. "Oh, man. I don't have to go to a doctor, do I? I could go to some free clinic, so my parents won't find out?"

"If you're positive, your parents are going to have to know."

"But I just have to take some pills, right?"

"For the rest of your life, Theo. If you're positive, you'll never be able to have unprotected sex again. Even if you get married. If you want to have kids you'd have to go through procedures to make sure don't pass it on to them."

"But I could be okay? It was only the one time."

"You could be." I sat back against the fancy sofa. "How'd you know her, if you go to Punahou, and she went to McKinley?"

He looked up. "My cousin goes to McKinley. I must have met her through him."

"Your cousin's name?"

"You won't tell him I gave you his name, will you?"

"Theo. Give me his name, or I wait until your parents come home and ask them."

"Joe," he said. "Joe Mishima." Suddenly, the words were spilling out. "He had sex with her, and he told me she'd do it with me, too. He gave me her profile name on WhatsApp, and he told me create a fake profile, and what to say to her."

Joe Mishima. Hadn't we spoken to him at McKinley? I'd have to check. "Do you know what his profile name was?" I asked.

"SekushiPenisu."

*A teenage boy calling himself Sexy Penis in Japanese? Give me a break.* But I did remember that one from Laney's list of contacts.

He leaned forward. "Please don't tell my parents. They'll freak out. You don't know what it's like, all this pressure to do well in school, be active in all kinds of groups, get into a good college. If my parents find out they'll lock down everything and all I'll have is school. I'll go crazy."

I knew the kind of pressure he referred to; I'd felt it from my parents, and I'd seen what my brothers were doing to their kids. That didn't excuse his behavior, though. I got his cousin's address from Theo and left, with a warning to get himself tested for all kinds of STDs, pronto.

From my notes, I saw that Ray and I had spoken to Joe Mishima earlier that day. He was the one who thought someone did the world a favor by killing Laney.

The address Theo had given me was only a few blocks away, but it was on the other side of a street that divided rich from poor. Joe's house was on the poor side, and I wondered what that was like for him, having rich relatives so close, with a cousin who went to an expensive private school.

An elderly man answered the door, and after I showed him my badge he identified himself as Joe's grandfather. "He's not here. He and his brother left this afternoon. Went up to the North Shore for a few days."

"In the middle of the school year?" I asked, though I figured it was our conversation at McKinley that had prompted the departure.

The man shrugged. "Their father ran off years ago, and their mother, my daughter, died two years ago. Since they come to live with me, they are nothing but trouble. They don't listen to anything."

He allowed me in the house to check, and led me to the small room Joe shared with his brother Walt. The walls were festooned with surfing posters, the way mine had been when I was a teenager. There were decals from Town & Country Surf Shop, Sexwax, and a bunch of other stores and products stuck to every surface.

"Hmph," the grandfather snorted. "Their father should never have taught them to surf. They run away like this whenever the waves get big."

We walked back out to the living room, where I saw a pair of school photos on the table by the sofa. "These recent?" I asked.

"Close enough," the grandfather said. "School pictures from last year."

I asked if I could borrow the pictures, and the grandfather agreed. On my way home I called Ray and filled him in on what I'd discovered. "You want to go up to the North Shore and look for them now?" he asked.

"Easier to do in daylight," I said. "We'll start at Haleiwa Beach Park and keep going until we find them."

When I got home I logged into the department's computer system and put out a BOLO—be on the lookout—for Joe Mishima's grandfather's car, with instructions to call me if it was spotted. Then Mike came home and we barbecued burgers on the grill, hanging out with Dakota and trying to pretend the world wasn't a deadly place for teenagers.

The next morning Ray picked me up and we took the H2 until it died out into the Kam by Schofield Barracks. From there it was two lanes up over the hump of the island, most of the traffic heading in the same direction, toward the waves of the North Shore.

Ray's was one of the few vehicles without one or more surfboards lashed to the roof or standing up in the back of pickups. It had been too long since I'd been out on a good wave, and I missed it. But today was all about work, tormenting myself with fast breaks while we searched for a teenaged boy who might have the key to a murder.

There were no parking spots at Haleiwa Beach Park, so we cruised slowly around the lot looking for Joe Mishima's car. Didn't find it, so we continued up to Lanikea and then Chun's Reef. It wasn't hard to go slowly enough to check out the cars parked alongside the road; everybody seemed to be cruising along looking for parking.

We were just approaching Waimea Beach Park when my cell

rang. A uniform had spotted Joe's car parked near Velzyland, the easternmost of the North Shore breaks, and was keeping an eye on it until we arrived.

"I know you live for this," I said to Ray, reaching into his glove compartment for the portable police light. "Uniform spotted Joe's car. We've got to move."

He rolled down his window and used one hand to slot it into the roof mount. I plugged the cord into the cigarette lighter. Then the light was going, and we were zooming around all the slow traffic on the Kam.

"You been to this break before?" Ray asked, as we hit a clear patch of roadway.

"Yeah. Very localized break—not big with tourists. Strong currents, dangerous reef. You really need to know what you're doing to surf up there."

We reached the small parking lot by the beach and spotted the cruiser. Ray turned off the light and we coasted up beside the uniform.

"Fourth car in from the end," he said, pointing at the lot. "Haven't seen anyone come or go from it since I spotted it."

"Good eyes," I said. "Thanks. You'll hang around?"

"Happy to oblige. There's a wide spot up there about three hundred feet—you can park there."

Ray slotted the big SUV into the narrow space with expertise learned on the narrow streets of Philadelphia. I grabbed a pair of high-powered binoculars I'd brought, and we walked down the sand toward the beach. I had the photos of Joe Mishima and his brother Walt, and we scanned the beach but didn't see them.

I pulled out the binoculars and focused on the surfers out beyond the break, waiting for the next wave. I spotted Joe Mishima prone on a board, paddling lightly to keep his place, and handed the glasses to Ray. "The big guy on the short board," I said.

Ray spotted him and then handed the glasses back to me. We

watched as a wave built behind Joe and he began paddling like mad to catch the lip. "Don't see how you guys do that," Ray said. "Looks just crazy to me."

"Crazy fun," I said, as Joe stood up with the sun on him, looking like I imagined my Hawaiian ancestors might have, long before these shores were colonialized and commercialized.

"How big do you think that wave is?" Ray asked.

"Probably top out about eight feet," I said. "If he's surfing this break he ought to be able to handle it."

Joe Mishima was good, moving his body in time with the water, crouching, standing, shifting his balance as the water flowed under him. He wasn't quite good enough, though, and he tumbled off the board into the churning water.

"There's a coral reef below there," I said to Ray. "If Joe isn't careful he's going to get cut up pretty badly."

There was nothing we could do but stand there and watch the water, hoping Joe would pop up. I looked a few feet down the beach and recognized his younger brother, watching the same place we were.

"Keep an eye out," I said to Ray, and I walked over to the kid. He looked familiar, and I realized that I had seen both boys at the mini-park on Monday morning, when Laney's body had been found.

"You're Walt Mishima," I said to him. I pegged him at about fifteen, around the same awkward break between kid and adult as Dakota. I showed him my badge. "Detective Kanapa'aka, HPD."

I'd barely gotten the words out of my mouth when he took off up the sand. He was barefoot, which gave him a better purchase on the sand, but I'd been running on beaches since I was a kid and I knew how to place my feet. I caught up to him and grabbed his arm.

"Hey! Let the kid go!" A burly Hawaiian guy bigger than my brother Haoa started toward us. "You some kind of freak?"

A couple of surfers started to gather around us as I reached into my pocket for my badge. "Some kind of cop," I said, glad that I wasn't even winded. "Good to see you guys watch out for each other. Keep it up."

"He don't have to go with you," the big guy said.

"You want to come with us?" I asked. "Down to headquarters in Honolulu? Maybe you helped this guy and his brother murder a sixteen-year-old girl?"

The uniform had joined us by then. "Cuff him and put him in your car," I said. The uniform pulled his cuffs out.

"Anybody else?" I asked. "Accessory after the fact on a homicide charge can keep you off the beach for a while."

The surfers faded back to their boards and their blankets and I walked back to Ray. He was watching Joe Mishima struggle up the beach, his forehead bleeding.

"Hey, Joe," I said, as we walked up to him. "They say third time's a charm, right? First time we saw you was outside the park where Laney Kahika died. Then at McKinley yesterday, now here." I pulled my cuffs off my belt. "We've got to stop meeting like this."

"Where's my brother?" he asked.

"Already in police custody," I said. "Turn around."

He knew the drill. He turned his back to us and held out his wrists, and I cuffed him. "Walt didn't have anything to do with this," he said. "He was home in bed."

"Hold on, cowboy," I said. I read him his Miranda rights as we walked up the beach, the surfers clearing a path for us. Joe called to a friend to pick up his board, and Walt's.

I put Joe in the back of Ray's SUV and then slid in beside him. "You gotta keep Walt out of this," Joe said. "I'll tell you everything if you let my little brudda go free."

"Can't make any promises," I said. "Charging is up to the District Attorney. But you tell us your story, and we'll see what we can do."

Ray pulled out into traffic, with the uniform in his patrol car behind us.

Joe nodded. "It was all the bitch's fault," he said. "She got me sick. I didn't even know it until I took my physical for the Army. The nurse gets all serious with me, tells me I'm HIV positive. Had to be Laney."

"I'd be pissed off if I were you," I said, as Ray drove down the Kam toward Honolulu. "You talk to her about it?"

"Went to her house Sunday night. I knew her mom worked nights and she'd be home by herself."

"What happened then?"

"I got her to come out with me to the park. We drank and she zonked out."

"That when you called your brother to help you string her up, make her death look like a suicide?"

"I told you, leave Walt out of it. I did it all myself."

I couldn't blame him for trying to protect his brother; I'd do the same for either of mine. So I didn't press him, even though I knew we had fingerprints from two different individuals, and I was willing to bet they'd match Joe and Walt Mishima.

When we got back to headquarters, we took a full confession from Joe, and deliberately waited to speak to Walt until after the DA had spoken with Joe. "I can't let the brother off completely," the DA said. "But I can bargain him down to something where he'll get probation and counseling."

I was on my way home that night, tired and depressed, when my nephew Alec called me. "Hey, Uncle K," he said.

"You can't have used up that whole box of condoms so fast," I said, only half joking.

"Haven't used any of them," he said. "Theo told me that he talked to you."

"You don't have to listen to me," I said. "I'm just your uncle. But I don't think Theo's the kind of friend you want to hang around with too much."

"He's not a bad guy, Uncle K," Alec said. "But after seeing what kind of trouble he got into I think I'm going to keep it in my pants for a while longer."

"It won't fall off if you do," I said. "The condoms will expire eventually. But if they do, and you still haven't used them, I'm happy to replace them with a new box."

"Thanks, Uncle K," said. "You're the best."

I didn't know about that, but for a brief moment I felt pretty good.

# Acknowledgements

A big shout-out to my Hawaiian 'ohana, who give me advice and keep Kimo's world real. My editor, Kris Jacen; librarian extraordinaire Cindy Chow, a friend to mystery writers and mystery lovers; and mystery authors Deborah Turrell Atkinson and Annette Mahon (who appears under her maiden name in one of the stories).

Other awesome writers who have helped and inspired me are Vicki Hendricks and Anthony Bidulka. Thank you to Dan Jaffe for giving Kimo his first venture into print. Miriam Auerbach, Christine Jackson, Christine Kling, Kris Montee and Sharon Potts are not only terrific writers but great critique group partners.

The Staff and Program Development department at Broward College has supported my work, allowing me to travel to conferences from England to Hawaii and many places in between, and my long-ago employers at GameTek gave me the chance to spend a lot of time in San Francisco, getting to know the Castro and all the sights that inspired Kimo in "Kelly Green."

Marc, Brody and Griffin all keep things interesting for me, providing me with inspiration (and often an incentive to get out of the house and get writing!).

"Refuge" originally appeared in *Blithe House Quarterly*. "Other People's Children" first appeared in certain editions of *Natural Predators*, published by MLR Press.

2006

*Mahu* – September-October

*Mahu Surfer* – October - November

"I Know What You Did" – November

"Blowing It" – November

"Christmas in Honolulu" – December

2007

"The Price of Salt" – January

"Super-Size" – January

"Online, Nobody Knows You're A Dog" – February

"The Cane Fields" – March

"Sex in Salt Lake" – March

*Mahu Fire* – April

"The Sun God and the Boy He Loved" – June

"The Whole Ten Million" – July

"A Rainy Day at Black Point" – November

"The Second Detective" – November

2008

"False Assumptions" – January

"Island Ball" – February

"Mahu Dating" – March

"Accidental Contact" – April

"Kelly Green" – May

"Paniolo" – June

"Refuge" – July

"Slamming the Poet" – August

*Mahu Vice* – October November

2009

"Mr. Surfer" – January

"A Shaggy Dog Story" – March

"Lomi-Lomi Massage" – April

*Mahu Blood* -         August - September

"Macadamia Nuts to You" – October

2010

"Body Removal" – August

"Missionary Road" – November

2011

*Zero Break* -March

"The Burning Woman"  - June

2012

"Other Peoples' Children" – January

*Natural Predators* – March

"Alpha and Omega" – December

2013

"Transmission" – January

*Ghost Ship* – February

NEIL PLAKCY is the author of *Mahu, Mahu Surfer, Mahu Fire, Mahu Vice, Mahu Men, Mahu Blood,* and *Zero Break* about openly gay Honolulu homicide detective Kimo Kanapa'aka. His other books include the *Have Body, Will Guard* series, the *Golden Retriever Mysteries*, and numerous stand-alone works of romance and mystery. His website is www.mahubooks.com.

The author acknowledges the trademark status and trademark owners of the following wordmarks mentioned in this work of fiction:

7-Eleven: 7-Eleven, Inc.

Actifed: Johnson & Johnson

Alan Wong: Alan Wong's Restaurants

Bank of Hawai'i: Bank of Hawaii

Berkeley: UC Regents

Brooks Brothers: Brooks Brothers Group, Inc.

Children's Discovery Center: Hawaii Children's Discovery Center

Claritin-D: MSD Consumer Care, Inc.

ContacMeda: Consumer Health Care Inc.

Delta: Delta Air Lines, Inc.

Doc Martens: Dr. Martens AirWair USA LLC

Facebook: Facebook

FedEx: FedEx

First Hawaiian Center: First Hawaiian Bank

Ford: Ford Motor Company

Glock: Glock, Inc.

Google Maps: Google

Hawaiian Heritage Jewelry: Royal Hawaiian Jewelry

Hello Kitty: Sanrio Co., Ltd.

Honda Accord: American Honda Motor Co., Inc.

Jeep: Chrysler Group LLC

Jiffy Pop: ConAgra Foods, Inc.

K-Y: McNEIL-PPC, Inc.

Lilo and Stich: Disney

Long's: Long's Drugs

Longboard LagerKona Brewing Co.

Macy's: Macy's Inc.

Mazzei Badiola: Palm Bay International

Mucinex-D: Reckitt Benckiser

Nissan Sentra: Nissan Motor Co., Ltd.
Pleasure Pack: Church & Dwight Co., Inc.
Punahou: Punahou School
Rolodex: none
Salvation Army: The Salvation Army
Sears: Sears Brands
Sex Wax: Sexwax, Inc.
Smith & Wesson: Smith & Wesson
Spam: Hormel Foods, LLC
Star-Advertiser: Star Advertiser
Starbucks: Starbucks Corporation
Sudafed: McNEIL-PPC, Inc.
Swiss Army Knife: Victorinox
Tarzan: Edgar Rice Burroughs, Inc.
Town & Country Surf Shop: Town & Country Surf
Toyota and Highlander: Toyota Motor Sales USA
University of Hawaii: The University of Hawaii
Vicks Vapo-Rub: Trademark Expired
Ward Center: The Howard Hughes Corporation
WhatsApp: WhatsApp Inc
YMCA: YMCA of the USA
Zyrtec-D: McNEIL-PPC, Inc.

CPSIA information can be obtained
at www.ICGtesting.com
Printed in the USA
LVHW02s0619030518
575815LV00001B/4/P